Catalyst

Cat's Crusade
Book 1

Nik Morton

ROUGH
EDGES
PRESS

Rough Edges Press
An Imprint of Wolfpack Publishing
9850 S. Maryland Parkway, Suite A-5 #323
Las Vegas, Nevada 89183

roughedgespress.com

Paperback ISBN 978-1-68549-237-3
eBook ISBN 978-1-68549-236-6

To Jennifer, with love, as always, for always.
And to Hannah, Harry, Darius and Suri.

cat•a•lyst (ˈkæt-l-ɪst)

n.

1. a substance that causes or speeds a chemical reaction without itself being affected
2. a person or thing that precipitates an event or change

Ananke

The name of a primordial deity in Greek mythology, the personification of necessity and fate. She was present when the universe began, with her consort, Chronos (time). She was said to rule over fate. Being the mother of the Fates, only she could control their decisions.

Catalyst

Chapter 1

Cat Among the Pigeons

June 2014—London

Rock climbing was much easier than this, Cat Vibrissae thought. She did free climbing for a hobby—though only in daylight—and enjoyed it. But climbing the outside of a modern building at night was something else entirely. She was used to the adrenaline rush of climbing with bare hands and feet on cliffs above rugged rocks and aggressive waves. But this was so very different. Tonight, her physiological responses seemed more pronounced: she was sure that she could sense her increased heart rate and her gut constricting. And her mouth was exceedingly dry. Still, if she was going to fulfill her vow to her late father, she had no choice. This was the only way to penetrate the seventeenth-floor office of Rick Barnes.

Finding handholds on the face of a modern building was not easy at the best of times but, at night, it was worse and had to be done by feel alone. Street lighting and advertising signs didn't help this high up—but at least the darkness ensured she wouldn't be visible. Here, she would find no holes made by burrowing animals or nesting birds. Simply rigid straight edges of concrete and marble and no potentially unsafe cladding, fortunately. Clean lean lines as envisioned by the architects. God, how she would dearly love to hammer pitons into the stone facade and secure a few karabiners and snap-rings and rope, but that would make an unacceptable amount of noise and, besides, it would take far too long. But the ropes would have eased the strain on her fingers, wrists, arms, and legs.

Stop moaning. Just get on with it.

If she hadn't also done plenty of free climbing, she'd never have contemplated this. Her coach had used the phrase, "Make the geckos jealous." Unfortunately, she didn't have suction-pad feet. At least her soft Five Ten Anasazi climbing shoes acted like "magic fingers" and enabled her feet to cling to the narrowest of ledges and feel the features she stepped on.

When she started this climb, the air had been quite calm, not too balmy, an ideal June evening, with hardly a breeze disturbing her long auburn ponytail. Refreshing, even. But now, fifteen stories up, the swirling air currents tugged at her slim-line backpack and black cat-suit and threatened to blow her off the side of the building. Specks of dust and leaves flicked against her cheeks; she was really glad she wore wrap-around goggles.

Toe tips only. Using her toes and not her instep allowed her hips a broader moving range to allocate her gravity center as needed. The technique required her to move her hips over her feet. "Follow gravity", her coach had said. "The hip is the center of gravity." Simple, really. Placing her hip over one foot relieved both her other foot and her hands for the next move. And so on.

Keep calm.

She passed behind the huge metal sign for ANANKE CORPORATION which, thankfully, wasn't illuminated at this time of night.

Here, she decided to rest for a few minutes and looped a leg over a stanchion and suddenly she gave a start as two disturbed pigeons flapped their wings and flew out and away, leaving behind a stomach-churning stink of bird droppings. At least the bird-flu scare had long since petered out; and since pigs can't fly, there was no risk of swine flu either. *Ha, ha...*

The inane joke didn't calm her, though. After that shock, her heart was fluttering more than ever.

Two days ago, it had been pounding for a different reason.

———

CAT'S HEART quickened as Rick Barnes let her into his Richmond apartment and shut the door behind them. She brushed her slightly clammy hands down her maroon pleated skirt. This was the culmination of two weeks' dating, waiting for the right time to accept his invitation to stay overnight.

His gray-blue eyes glinted in the light from the chandelier. He seemed particularly dashing tonight in his black tux and bow tie. "Yet another wonderful meal —thanks to your company, of course."

"Of course," she said playfully.

How gallant. He smiled with slightly moist thick lips, lips she'd tasted on several occasions at her own rented apartment's threshold. She had refrained from commenting on his rather large beaked nose, even though it was difficult to avoid. He almost gave her a black eye when they first kissed. It gave him a predatory aspect, but it was she who regarded him as her prey.

The wall-mounted telephone by the door rang. "Cathy, can you pour us brandy while I get that?" he said and moved toward it.

"Love to." She strode over to the drinks cabinet and fingered her elaborate Victorian-style signet ring. This was too good an opportunity to miss, she reasoned.

He lifted the phone, listened, and spoke briefly. "I won't forget, Loup," he said. "Don't worry. No, of course you don't. The land purchase is going ahead, as planned." He replaced the receiver and sighed.

At hearing the mention of Loup, Cat felt her legs tremble ever so slightly. So near... She removed the stopper from the Courvoisier bottle. Her stomach was involved in some kind of African tribal dance, she felt sure. What she was about to attempt was high-risk. Was it anticipation or fear that sent her senses scattering haywire?

As Rick walked over to her, Cat smiled and turned her back to him. Deftly, she placed her signet ring over his glass, opened the lid, and spilled the fine, powdery contents, and then shut the lid. She poured a generous measure of the liquor into both glasses, swirling it around to dissolve the powder in his glass.

She turned to face him. His glass, she reminded herself, was in her left hand.

"It's nice to see you have a good appetite," he said, walking toward her, "not like most models I've met."

"I don't subscribe to that size zero nonsense."

"So I see."

She chuckled, liking his forthright appraisal of her. "I find that constantly walking up and down and quickly changing into fresh clothes burns enough calories." She handed him his glass.

"Thanks. It was a good show," he said.

"It was. Not too hectic. February was murder, fashion weeks in both Madrid and Milan! Do you go to many clothes shows?"

Exasperatingly, he didn't bother drinking from it but eyed her, instead. "I like beautiful women, so sue me."

She said nothing, simply sipped her brandy. The fiery liquid burned her tongue and sent tiny prisms of pleasure cascading around her mouth. She licked her lips, and they tingled as she looked at him over the glass rim. "All week, you've flattered me. I've never been chased before."

His thick dark eyebrows arched. "I'm surprised. Anyway, I also invest in a few clothes designers if I like their stuff. I noticed a few there tonight. Christopher Bailey from Burberry—and also Julien MacDonald and Matthew Williamson." He grinned. "I like to spread my portfolio, you know?"

"Models aren't part of your portfolio, are they?"

He laughed, a warm deep sound, and ran a hand through his thick black hair. "No, of course not. I took a liking to you. A strong liking." He clinked his glass against hers but didn't drink. "It seems to be mutual. Call it fate or chemistry, if you like."

"Oh, definitely chemistry," she said.

"Yes. I think we get on really well, don't you?"

She nodded. "Otherwise I wouldn't be here."

"Just so."

Infuriatingly, he still hadn't taken as much as a sip from his glass.

"That's a delightful perfume you're wearing tonight, Cathy."

"You like it?"

"Oh, yes."

Rick sipped his brandy. *At last!* She willed him to drink all of it.

"*Manifesto Rossellini,*" he announced, "if I'm not mistaken."

"I'm impressed." She was amused, despite herself. "Most men haven't got a clue about fragrances."

"My secretary, Mandy, she always uses *L'instant de Guerlain.*" He tilted the glass back, downed its contents, and put the glass on the cabinet. *Finally.*

Then he shrugged out of his jacket and slung it on the back of a chair by the mahogany desk.

She wondered if she'd find what she wanted in his desk's drawers. *Doubtful.* "Really?"

"Yes." He loosened his black bow tie and then fumbled with his waistcoat buttons. "I haven't come across *Rossellini* in a long time, actually." He moved near and she didn't falter, her rump pressed against the edge of the drinks cabinet.

Rick leaned his head forward so that his nose was just above the hollow of her neck. Her ultramarine designer blouse was opened to show off her cleavage, but she noted he was enough of a gentleman to close his eyes as he sniffed delicately. "Hmm, it suits you."

"Thanks," she said, gratified. She'd been diligent in preparing for this night's seduction, starting with a shower and body spray then applying the perfume on her lower body and working her way up to her wrist, neck, and cleavage, where it would stay warm longer and be more effective. That's what customers paid for: the aroma of expensive perfume lingered longer than cheap varieties.

He stepped back a pace and opened his eyes. "Allow me?" he asked, reaching out to the topmost fastened button of her blouse.

Cat put down her nearly full glass, the corners of her mouth twitching in anticipation. She studied his face as he unbuttoned the blouse. His lashes were long and fine. The touch of his hands as they brushed against her seemed to send electrical charges through her entire body.

"Should I stop?" he asked. "I haven't got my signals crossed, have I?"

"No, don't stop. Me, I never got my Girl Guide semaphore badge..." She raised a hand and ran it over his craggy features. It made a faint rasping sound. His firm jaw was already prickly with fresh stubble.

His steely gaze was penetrating. "I'm not quite the Boy Scout tonight, am I?"

Cat shook her head and smiled. "Maybe I can award you a badge of some sort." She eased her arms out of the blouse and gently threw it on top of his jacket. Its sheer luminosity had evoked some gasps from the side of the catwalk earlier in the evening, she recalled. "We'll see, later."

"No hurry for later. I like now." Rick kissed her neck, his big hands brushing over the lace cups of her ivory Lise Charmel bra.

She felt her nipples respond, becoming hard nubs against the fabric.

"You're good," she whispered.

"I'd rather be bad."

She pulled his bow tie free and discarded it behind her. "The night's young yet." She kissed him, her nose knocking against his.

"Sorry, it's me," he whispered, tapping a big finger against the side of it. "As you've found already, it's rather large," he confessed, "but it means that I'm blessed with an acute sense of smell."

"Like that fellow in the book *Perfume*?"

"I hope not. He murdered virgins to obtain the perfect scent, didn't he?"

He not only reads books but remembers what he has read, she thought. Cat almost felt sorry for him. Almost. "Well, I've got nothing to fear, since I'm not a virgin."

He put his hands on her shoulders. "I won't respond to that—save to say, you've been divine all week, just like your scent."

"Thank you. But why are you a company lawyer, when you could work for any perfume conglomerate you fancied?"

"Actually, I offer my services to the Ananke chemists in Barcelona when they come up with a new fragrance."

I know. That's why I'm here! "Big nose, big hands," she said in an amused tone, glancing past the noticeable bulge in his trousers to his patent black leather shoes.

"Yes, big feet too." His eyes shone, amused. "It's true what they say, Cathy." He embraced her with powerful arms, his body's firmness enticing.

Her fingers unfastened his shirt buttons, and they slid inside, brushing his chest hair. With immense

8

effort, she resisted the overwhelming warmth that suffused her. "Not here, Rick." She kissed him then gently eased away and raised an eyebrow. "Shall we go where it's more comfortable?"

"Yes, good idea." He grinned and enveloped her hand in his.

He led her across the room to a door and opened it.

The bedroom was huge, with a king-size bed.

He stifled a yawn.

"Am I keeping you up?" she asked.

"Oh, decidedly," he replied, his eyes dancing playfully, acknowledging the double entendre. He swept her up into his arms and walked through the doorway.

She hoped he wouldn't succumb right now and drop her, or worse, collapse on top of her.

Then he lowered her to the bed which was quite firm with only a slight bounce. "Comfortable enough for you?" he queried.

"It's lovely, Rick." She raised her arms and put her hands behind her head. She kicked off her high-heeled shoes and they fell to the floor.

"And so are you," he said, gazing at her.

He has all the right words. Pity he's Mr. Wrong.

Rick hastily tugged his shirt out of his waistband and up over his head. It joined her shoes on the carpet. His muscles rippled.

Abruptly, his eyes glazed over, and she rolled out of the way moments before he slumped face down onto the bed at her side, his legs dangling over the edge.

Nearly pinned under him! That might have been awkward.

Her pulse racing, Cat slid off the bed. She needed freedom of movement which her skirt would not allow, so she unzipped it and stepped out of it. Then she climbed back on the bed and hooked her hands under Rick's hairy armpits. Straining, she began hauling him fully onto the mattress. It was difficult as there was little purchase and she was inclined to bounce. She was soon sweating with exertion.

Finally, he lay entirely on the bed.

He made a slight snuffling sound but otherwise didn't stir. She was confident that he wouldn't wake—she'd been very careful and given him only enough powder to knock him out for about five hours. She unfastened his belt and, after a slight struggle, pulled off his trousers. A mischievous part of her was tempted to tug off his marine blue Michael Kors boxer briefs to verify the adage he'd alluded to, but she refrained. It seemed wrong since she'd drugged him.

Kneeling beside him, she thought he was certainly a fine specimen of manhood, his broad chest clustered with hair, his torso and arms muscular and toned. Sighing at what might have been, Cat managed to shove him under the sheets.

She swung her legs off the bed, stood, picked up her skirt, and walked into the lounge where she retrieved her blouse from the ladder-backed chair. She buttoned up the blouse and put on the skirt; the pleats draped without a crease. Then she put on her shoes and knelt beside his jacket that was draped over the chair.

Her pulse rate increased as she pulled out his billfold. The usual credit and debit cards, a Durex sachet, a credit card-sized calculator, and a photograph of a woman and two young girls—probably his wife and daughters, the damned cheat... Then, tucked tightly against the lining, she spotted a thin slip of paper. She read and memorized the number sequence. It looked like a security code—either for the computer or a digital safe. A few days earlier, over dinner, Rick had confessed that he was hopeless at remembering passwords and codes, which had convinced her that tonight's seduction was worth the risk. And so it was, she realized. Her heart raced because she was finally in a position to begin in earnest her campaign against the Ananke Corporation. Angers in France had been merely a warm-up exercise—in more ways than one.

Rick knew her as Cathy Gledhill, the name she adopted for her modeling work. Cat on the catwalk. She had been lumbered with the sobriquet "Cat" at the convent school and it had stuck. Her father had hated it. To him, she was always Catherine, never Cathy or Cate.

When she had stood in front of her father's open coffin in his village church, she'd fought back the tears. Her chest had felt fit to explode but somehow she'd controlled herself. Although she knew that the fatal car crash hadn't damaged his face at all, she was still surprised at how serene he looked, as though he was simply asleep, leathery cheeks about to rise and fall with shallow breathing, his thick bushy gray hair surrounding his head as usual, like a halo. She had half-expected his unkempt mustache to twitch as it did when he was about to laugh, his hazel eyes sparkling with mischief. But his eyes were closed. Bending over him, she had kissed his cold forehead for the last time and vowed to destroy those who had brought him to grief.

THE WIND UP here must have blown something in her eyes; she raised a finger to wipe the moisture away and its tip bumped against the goggles. Instead, she blinked her eyes clear of stinging tears evoked by memories.

The sweat at the base of her spine had dried and she felt a slight chill over her kidneys. *Time to get moving*.

Heaving a big sigh, she started climbing again—only two more stories to go.

Finally, she reached the window ledge of Rick's office and carefully pulled herself up. Sitting here, her legs dangling, she paused to admire the view and regain some strength in her limbs.

The cityscape was beautiful, lights of varying shades of yellow glinting. Like fairy lights. The office block opposite was illuminated in parts, like a half-completed advent calendar offering an insight into other secret lives; in some windows, she could see a few dedicated souls working late; in one she glimpsed a couple lying on the top of the conference table, indulging in unspecified overtime that entailed divesting their clothing. She envied them their sense of abandon but not the deceit that probably went with it. She didn't like the lying that her vow made necessary but accepted the need for it. The end justifies the means? She believed it did.

She briefly thought of Rick lying in his bed and was surprised at experiencing a feeling of guilt.

Mentally shaking herself, Cat turned to the uPVC window. Clearly, Rick and his staff didn't think much about climate change or wasting energy, as all the overhead lights were on. His office was large, with an enormous expanse of fawn-colored carpet and a wide walnut desk. There was the computer, in power-save mode, and a printer on top of a wooden cupboard. On the opposite wall was a framed portrait of the head of Ananke.

She guessed that when he posed for that portrait, Loup Dante was about ten years younger; he was now sixty-three. Cat recognized him from the countless photographs in *Fortune* and other business periodicals. Pasty complexion, dun-colored eyes and pencil-width whiskers that extended from the bottom lip to the cleft chin. His mustache was the waxed type, curled at the tips. He looked supercilious and untrustworthy, maintaining a thin smile that concealed yellowed teeth.

Windows this high up wouldn't be alarmed, for obvious reasons. Many modern offices were not fitted with opening windows, relying on climate-control systems to maintain a constant temperature. Fortunately, this wasn't one of them: the opening section was the top half.

Still sitting on the window ledge, Cat unfastened the large suction cup from the back of her belt. It was designed to pull out dents in car bodywork. She reached up and placed the rubber against the center of the bottom half of the window and closed the clamps; it gripped tightly and wouldn't budge. She clipped the suction cup's rope to a snap-ring on her waist and slowly stood up, her knees beginning to wobble. Primordial fear of heights—endowed through genes since we'd all lived in trees, she told herself—threatened to plunge her out and down.

Even with the security of the line attached to the suction cup, the sweat of fear beaded her forehead. *Totally irrational.* Strangely, she never experienced this anxiety when free climbing. Hard pavement was no worse than jagged rocks. Perhaps it was the idea of the city itself. Rocks and mountains seemed more natural.

She resisted the instinctive response to close her eyes. That would disorient her and definitely send her out into space where she'd really test the strength of the suction cup.

Focusing on the window frame, she slowly unclipped a screwdriver from her belt and wedged it in the join between frame and window. Careful not to lean back, she applied weight precisely and forced the window catch. She replaced the screwdriver and lifted open the window.

Her hazy reflection in the window revealed a couple of dead leaves on her shoulder. Standing quite steady, she brushed the street dust and leaves off her shoulders, arms, and knees with her hands. She didn't want any tell-tale signs to be discovered on the fawn carpet of the office.

From a belt-pouch, she withdrew a pair of light latex gloves and put them on then checked the other belt-pouches and the waterproof canvas bag—all secure.

Everything must have a place.

"You must keep your room tidy, Catherine, dear," her mother had said more than once. "I won't always be here to clear up." Prophetic words, indeed.

After her mother was taken away by the very disease her father's products were being tested to cure, Cat incessantly cleaned and tidied the house, constantly asking her father, "Will Maman come back, now that I have been good?" She lost her mother when she was seven and persisted in being obsessed about tidiness and cleanliness until her teens when her father's doctor friend finally helped her to pull out of it.

Patience and love helped, too, of course.

Now, she played out sufficient slack in the rope and hauled herself up through the window. As she twisted around, gripping the frame for support, some metal tools clanged against the glass but there was nobody to hear.

She eased her legs in, careful not to snag the harness of her slim-line backpack.

Once on the interior sill, she unclipped the rope and jumped to the floor, landing lightly on the thick pile.

She turned to check the inside windowsill and the carpet around her feet. No give-away marks or scuffs, no leaves or specks of dust. She slowly let out her breath.

Leaning on the desk, she moved the mouse over the pad and instantly brought the desktop screen back to life. As expected, he hadn't set up a password. Why bother when you have a secure office environment?

It didn't take long to find the financial and personnel files. She took out a memory stick from her belt pouch and inserted it into the USB port. Should be a doddle. But the flash drive wasn't recognized. Damn! Incompatible, of all things.

Her mouth was very dry, a sign of stress that she normally associated with extreme sports rather than using a computer. Still, this was her first burglary.

She put the memory stick away. She had no alternative, so she sent the relevant files to the printer, selecting the draft print option to speed things up.

While the inkjet was churning away, she checked the rest of the room.

An alarm console was beside the door and next to it was a single walnut filing cabinet, which didn't even have a lock, probably because that would have spoiled the appearance. Inside the top drawer were five files that interested her:

- COSMETICS—TESTING
- PLASTICS & BIODEGRADABLES —MANUFACTURING
- DRUGS—VARIOUS
- JEWELRY—ACQUISITIONS
- UNDERWATER RESEARCH

She recognized at least a couple of the titles—she was presently printing details about them from the computer files. At the risk of duplication, she decided she'd come back to these. For now, her prime reason for the break-in beckoned.

As she had hoped, the safe was behind the portrait of Loup Dante.

Brilliant! The four-digit code she'd found in his bill-fold opened it. She breathed a sigh of relief. Thanks, Rick...

She recalled yesterday's phone call from Rick. He'd been contrite. "I'm sorry you left before I woke up," he'd said.

She'd left a note. "I thought you seemed tired, so I sneaked out quietly," she whispered. "I've got an all-day shoot, so had to leave early." True enough.

"Oh." His tone was quite deflated.

"My taxi's waiting..."

"Right, I won't keep you, then. Can I call you again?"

"Of course." She'd sensed her heart flip at the prospect, even though he was working for the enemy. Besides, he might prove even more useful. "When I get back, we can make arrangements."

"I'd like that. And, Cathy, I'm really sorry. I'm afraid I don't know what happened, I don't normally—"

"Not to worry, Rick." *Let his ego down gently.* "It was a really lovely evening."

"Thanks," he said, and she'd hung up.

Grudgingly, she had to admit that she'd enjoyed her time with Rick, though he could be a little arrogant, but at least now her persistent efforts had proved worthwhile.

She opened the safe and immediately noticed a snub-nosed revolver and a wad of £50 notes. My God, was she getting involved in something too big? A gun, for God's sake! She forced herself to breathe steadily.

Taking the small Olympus digital camera out of her left-hand belt-pouch, she unclipped the lens cover and photographed the contents of the safe then checked the image—no blurring, it had come out fine.

Gingerly, she picked up the revolver. It was quite heavy, about two or three pounds in weight. On the left side of the barrel was the marking 'STURM RUGER & CO INC SOUTHPORT CONN USA'. On the right side, 'RUGER GP 100 .357 MAGNUM CAL'. What she surmised was the serial number had been scratched out, which suggested that it was stolen. The money amounted to £2,000. There was also a little green book and a folder with some incriminating photographs of Sebastian Dipple, a politician she recognized. There was another folder entitled CATANANCHE, which piqued her curiosity.

Cat went over to the desk light and switched it on. Unhurriedly, she photographed all the pages of the little green book, the sparse pages of the CATANANCHE folder, as well as the lewd photographs.

She was tempted to take the weapon and the money, but she didn't want Rick to suspect that anyone had invaded his office, let alone his safe. Using the digital photograph as a guide, she carefully replaced every item in the safe as she had found them, then closed and locked it.

She returned to the filing cabinet and removed the five files. There were far too many pages to photograph. She settled on the first half-dozen of each file, plus the indexes. Then she replaced the files as she found them, and shut the drawer

Almost done. She went over to pick up all the pages from the printer tray and put them in a waterproof canvas bag strapped to her shoulder, and then zipped it up.

With a few clicks of the mouse, the desktop screen was as she had found it; it would time-out to power-save mode shortly. Clicking on the lens-hood, she packed away the camera and gave the room a final visual check.

As she moved over to the windowsill, something nagged at the back of her mind, and she hesitated. *Double check.* She scanned the room again. Of course, the printer! She hadn't planned on using it, relying on the flash drive. *Careless.*

There were several reams in the cupboard under the printer and she broke one open and added roughly the same number of pages she'd printed on top of the blank sheets in the feed-tray. She reckoned that the ink usage wouldn't be noticed.

Satisfied now, Cat pulled herself up onto the sill and eased out of the window, reconnecting her waist-belt to the suction cup rope as she did so. She swung out and down, gingerly placing her feet on the outside sill. Then, taking a ball of blu-tack from another pouch, she squashed the putty-like substance against the catch and closed the window. The broken catch wouldn't be noticed until such time as someone tried to open the window, if ever.

Adrenaline was surging through her again as she unclamped the suction cup from the glass and secured it to her belt. Very carefully, she checked the harness and turned, her back to the window.

Now or never, she decided and thrust off from the relative security of the stone windowsill. It was disconcerting and shouldn't have been. She'd leaped from cliffs and mountainsides without any qualms, enjoying those exhilarating few seconds of free-fall. The unforgiving concrete below posed no greater danger.

One-hundred mile-per-hour wind-rush tugged at her face and clothes and adrenaline coursed through her. Every jump was subtly different, each one inde-scribable. After four seconds, Cat tugged open the extra-large gliding parachute that billowed from her backpack, the lines tugging at her harness and slowing her descent to about one thousand feet a minute.

With the ease borne of practice, she steered away from the buildings, toward the park. Street furniture and trees loomed up and then she passed them as her twelve-second parachute ride ended and, slightly breathless, she landed on the soft grass.

She bundled up the parachute and stowed it in a bag.

Cat was surprised at how elated she felt; her pulse was racing and her heart pounding. It had taken her four years to get to this point in her crusade. She intended to inflict a lot of damage on Ananke, and—armed with this new information—she would make them rue the day they steamrollered the Vibrissae family business.

———

SIX HOURS LATER, Rick Barnes opened his office door because he wanted to collect some papers for a meeting. Ignoring the alarm's beeping, he referred to a slip of paper pressed against the billfold in his free hand and deactivated the console.

As he moved over to Loup Dante's picture, Rick's nose twitched.

When he keyed in the combination of the safe, the same code as the door, he sniffed the air. "*Manifesto Rossellini,*" he mused and paused with his hand on the safe door. "Now, that *is* interesting," he said to the empty room.

Chapter 2

Cat and Mouse

"Petra Grimalkin," Rick said, "this is Cathy Gledhill, the model I told you about." He gestured at Cat. She was wearing a white satin full-length Emilio de la Morena dress with silver flowers glistening from her right shoulder, over her left breast to her narrow waist.

"Pleased to meet you, Miss Grimalkin." Cat unaccountably took an immediate strong dislike to the woman.

She was a statuesque brunette. "Do call me Petra."

As in the ancient city? Cat thought unkindly.

Cat thought Petra was an excellent role model for Ananke's cosmetics range, which was just as well since Petra headed up the Cosmetics Division. She wore a bright scarlet silk gown with pronounced shoulder pads shaped like roses. Cat couldn't identify the designer, but it was expensive. Petra was tall and big-boned with laser-like blue eyes surrounded by heavy, dark-blue liner. She held out her hand.

Firm and strong, Cat found. She offered a smile.

21

Petra curved carmine lips. "Rick has been eager for me to meet you. I absolutely loved that fashion shoot you did last month in the Seychelles. Even in those outrageous costumes, you looked gorgeous."

"Thank you," she said. *I think.*

Despite her charm and greeting, it seemed that Petra wasn't that keen to meet her, after all; she abruptly turned away with a hasty, "Excuse me. *Must* circulate!" flung over her tanned shoulder.

Good riddance—for now. "You'd think she was a magazine or something. Circulate, indeed!"

"She's a busy lady," Rick said.

"I can imagine."

"Put your claws back, darling," he whispered. "She's quite nice, really."

Cat chuckled. "I think she wouldn't like to know you reckon she's only 'quite nice'."

"No, I suppose not, and..." He faltered and pointed at the elevator doors as they glided open. "Ah, the boss has arrived."

Loup Dante, the head of Ananke stepped out of the cubicle and the talking stopped for a couple of beats. When it restarted, there seemed to be an indefinable layer of reticence in the volume and tone. Slowly, Cat allowed her own heart rate to slow. Seeing him in the flesh did strange things to her. She hadn't expected such a strong, gut-wrenching reaction. Gratefully, she sipped at the flute of chilled champagne.

Moments later, Rick led her away, introducing her to media types and serious businessmen.

After about forty minutes of moving around the room, Cat maneuvered herself and Rick to a position immediately behind Petra, who was chatting to Loup

Dante. It was not easy to eavesdrop while pretending to be attentive to a conversation with a buxom blonde TV presenter but she'd been to enough cocktail parties and end-shoot dos and had mastered the skill. After all, women were good at multi-tasking.

"I got the confirmation call ten minutes ago," Petra said. "Barcelona is at the final stage for the Catananche clinical tests."

Loup inclined his head. "Good—ahead of schedule, in fact. The EMA will be impressed. Very good."

Cat's ears seemed to prick up at the mention of Catananche. Earlier today, she'd read up on it from her downloaded pictures; not that there was much. Catananche was a drug undergoing clinical trials and currently with the European Medical Association's centralized new drug application process. Once the NDA was cleared, the drug was ready to go. But there was no clue in the documents as to what the drug actually did.

"I assume you will be going out there soon?" Petra said.

"Yes, I think it is time that I made a visit to see them. I've neglected them for the perfume branch, alas."

"Perfume makes you big bucks," Petra purred, "but Catananche will do much more. You know that. Do you want me to go with you?"

"Yes, that would be a good idea. Then, afterward, perhaps we can issue a press release."

"So soon?"

"My dear Petra, I assure you that once the EMA approves Catananche, this will be our license to print money."

He wasn't mistaken, either, Cat thought. She knew only too well how much money was to be made by pharma corporations. Yet instinctively she felt there was something amiss about the project. The test section of the report was simply a computer link, referring to a Profesora Quesada. Now, why was that?

"But that's enough talk about Catananche for now," Dante said. "Let's do a little more meet and greet, shall we?"

Abruptly, he turned and faced Cat.

Her heart seemed to skip a beat.

His facial appearance startled her. The left side of his face possessed a slight droop, the corner of his eye dragged down, the skin tight and glossy—the result of inadequate plastic surgery. Yet, his portrait didn't show this feature. And, of all the photographs she had seen of him, she now realized that he always presented his right side to the lens. His dun-colored eyes glinted in the overhead lighting and then, abruptly, widened momentarily. He held his head to one side, the left. She wondered if he had developed that mannerism since sustaining his facial deformity.

"This is Cathy Gledhill," Petra said. "She's with Rick."

Cat feared at any moment that she'd suffocate. Finally, she took in a breath and smiled, her mouth too dry to respond with a greeting.

"Charmed." His voice was soft and silky, but he didn't smile. He held out a hand.

Reluctantly, she shook hands. The clasp was even more firm than Petra's grip. His touch made her skin crawl. She hoped her repugnance wasn't conveyed in her eyes.·

His eyes narrowed, brow creased in thought. "Have we met before?" he asked, still retaining his grip on her hand.

She found her voice. "No," she said drily, "I'd have remembered."

She wanted to spit in his face, claw at his damned eyes, tear at his glossy skin and rip it from his skull. She retrieved her hand and barely refrained from wiping it on the folds of her dress.

"Perhaps you've seen Cathy's face on advertising hoardings?" Rick suggested.

"No..." Dante fingered the sparse whiskers at his chin. "Rather, I think...you remind me of someone." He seemed to force a smile as if saddened by a fleeting memory but didn't show his teeth. "No matter. I hope you enjoy the evening."

"I'm sure I shall," she said in a non-committal tone.

"Excuse us, please?" He turned, took Petra's elbow, and melted into the crowd.

Slowly, Cat let out a breath and unconsciously wiped her right hand on her dress. *Bastard!* She lifted the champagne flute to her lips and gratefully swallowed the entire contents to be rid of a dry bitter taste.

RICK TOOK Cat's empty glass and obtained two more drinks from a passing waiter. Something passed between Cat and Loup, he felt sure. And Petra had noticed it as well.

What were you up to in my office last night? More to the point, how the hell did you get in and circumvent the door-alarm? He'd asked the security doorman and he swore no woman answering Cathy's description had entered the building that evening. He wondered about the slip of paper with his combination numbers on it. Of course, she'd had ample opportunity to read it during his mysterious blackout. That was worrying, too. That hadn't happened to him in years—since college days, in fact. *Was she working for a rival firm?*

He had so many questions he wanted to ask her. Instead, he settled for the banal. "Quite a guy, isn't he?" He handed her a fresh glass.

"Thanks." She sipped and eyed him over the rim. "I'm sure he is, since he's head of a vast empire. I didn't get any feeling of charisma, though."

"How does that happen, 'the feeling of charisma'?"

She shrugged. "Certain people, when they enter the room, the world seems to stop for a few seconds. They can chat with you for a moment, and you feel you're the only one of importance to them. It's probably false, but it's definitely a real phenomenon. I've met a few. Only last month, I chatted with Daniel Craig on a shoot; he has it."

"You lead a glamorous life, Cathy. I think I envy you."

She shook her head. "Don't. Most of the time I'm in a make-believe world ruled by the airbrush and props. It's mostly boredom, hanging around a shoot, often with few clothes on, travel at ungodly hours, and meeting people I'd normally never want near me."

"Then why do it?"

"The money's good. It keeps me independent."

"Oh, does that mean you're not seeking a partner for life?"

"It does."

He sighed, tantalized by the memory of the moist kiss, his hands gliding over her bra, carrying her to the bed, and then—*blank*. "All right, I'll settle for tomorrow night, rather than life. Are you free then?"

"Sorry, I've got another shoot. This one's at night and, God help us, it's with animals."

Southampton

"It's raining cats and dogs out there. Southampton's not that pretty in sunshine but it's the pits when it rains!" Len Plummer fingered his brown and ginger mustache and stared above his rimless spectacles at the windshield. Even at high speed, the wiper blades barely permitted visibility through their arc of action; the downpour was so fierce.

"It's appropriate, then, isn't it," Cat joked.

He grunted. Len always tended to spout clichés when anxious. He'd become worse since giving up cigarettes. She was proud of him—he hadn't smoked for two months, apparently. There was no tell-tale smell on his clothing so she tended to believe him.

Their anonymous white Ford Transit van was parked some way distant from the nearest street lamp. Puddles glistened in the gutter and on the pavement.

Len pulled on his thick gloves. "I'm still game, if you are?" His thin lips curved, brown eyes scrutinizing her. "But you're going to get soaked."

"You're only sorry I'm not wearing a T-shirt," she said, grinning. They'd met during a fashion shoot. He and a handful of animal rights protesters had been

27

permitted to attend the show and they all calmed down when they discovered the models wore faux fur. Before they'd parted, he'd joked, "If you ever pose for a Pirelli calendar, let me know and I'll buy the entire stock!"

Now, she realized he was giving her this last chance to back out. Her mouth was dry and her stomach tumbled in anxiety. She pulled up her collar and hood and fastened the studs. "Let's do it."

"Right." He checked his voluminous canvas shoulder-bag, pulled the hood over his curly brown-ginger hair, and opened the driver's door. He stepped out and swore. "Sod it, I trod in a puddle!"

"It's your own fault, you should wear sensible shoes!"

"Hey, they're Nike. They set me back eighty quid!"

"Never mind," she said. "I'll buy you a new pair." Clasping a leather bag, she exited her side and they both quietly shut the doors. Her cheeks stung with the force of the rain. Despite her Craghoppers waterproof coat, trousers, and boots, within seconds of exposure to the elements, she felt cold, wet, and miserable. British weather, she hated it. Was it only last night that Petra reminded her of her fashion shoot in the Seychelles? *Seems a long way away—which it was—and a long time ago, which it wasn't.*

The building loomed dark and forbidding in the slanting rain. Somewhere, a strident car alarm blared. No security lights meant that Len's accomplice, Dolly, had successfully shut off the power supply.

They slunk past the innocuous notice proclaiming *Ananke Outlet 5, Southampton.*

"Follow me," Len whispered; she barely heard him above the downpour.

She raised an arm in acknowledgment. Rainwater streamed off her sleeve.

He led her along the wire fence, around the left-hand corner, level with the side of the building. Here, the darkness was deeper. Further from the streetlights.

She recalled Len's briefing—game plan, he called it: "Remember, we've got to move fast—fast and furious— and do what's necessary, then get out," he said. "We've got half an hour, tops, before their technician gets called out and restores the power."

She was glad she'd put on her Trespass boots; at least her feet were still dry and warm. An appropriate trade name, she mused, as Len withdrew his wire-cutters and fiercely snipped at the fence. Her water-proof hood and the pummeling rain drowned out most of the sound of the wire snapping.

Two minutes passed then Len's gloved hands peeled back the wire to provide a narrow access hole. "Not big enough to drive a coach and horses through, but it'll do." There was no point in concealing their entry—Ananke would know about the break-in soon enough. Gingerly, he stepped through the gap, clasping the bag against his chest to prevent it from snagging on one of the severed ends of the wire. She followed him without snagging her clothing or bag.

Len moved to the left, purposefully. According to the plan he'd shown her, there was a service entrance here, the door to the kitchens.

From his bag, he took out a hammer and a chisel and made short work of the lock: the door swung at the force of his final blow and the handle and lock clattered to the ground. Swiftly, he moved inside, and she was right behind him.

"Whew, that's better." He lowered his hood and shook his arms and torso. Rain droplets splashed to the tiled floor.

Len thrust the break-in tools into his bag then switched on a torch.

"Is it safe?" she asked.

He nodded, eyes glinting in the eerie light.

They were in a large kitchen area, the stainless-steel counters reflected his torch beam; also there were pots, pans and cooking utensils, refrigerators, and a walk-in freezer. There was a basic office desk, a filing cabinet, a couple of shelves of recipe books, and two aluminum chairs. Len closed the door and heaved a chair against it to keep it shut.

"Take a look." He aimed the torch beam behind her, at the high corner of the long kitchen. She turned. A CCTV camera lens pointed at the doorway they'd entered. She felt exposed and vulnerable under its glinting black glass eye. She was used to being filmed but not like this, caught in the act of breaking and entering.

"Power's out," he said, "so they don't function."

She released a sigh of relief. "That's pretty poor security, isn't it?" She lowered her own hood. "I'd have thought they'd put in fail-safes, a standby generator, in case there was a power-cut."

Len grinned and touched a finger to the side of his nose. "I know who installed the system. This little over-sight was deliberate. That's why we don't need bloody itchy balaclavas."

Taking out her own torch, she switched it on. "Where now?"

"This way."

Len led her through the right-hand doorway, out into a corridor. They trailed puddles behind them. As he strode ahead, his movement emitted a weird susurration from his clothing. He flashed the light beam at the doors on either side, finally stopping in front of the room labeled *Lab-A*.

"Bingo." He chuckled. "By God, I've been waiting for this for quite a while." He opened the door. She entered behind him and stepped to one side.

There was a distinct "pet shop" smell in the room and she was met by strange scuffling sounds. A dog growled in the shadows; the sound sent her stomach squirming. Quietly, she shut the door behind her. "Len?" she queried, apprehension in her voice.

"It's OK. There are no windows. Put the lights on."

She found the switch and flicked it.

Snarling, teeth bared, hackles up, the black mastiff covered the floor in swift loping strides.

Len held a pistol steady and fired.

A dart pierced the animal's chest and it tumbled heavily to the floor, coming to rest at her feet. "That's fast-acting," she managed.

"I'm surprised they keep him in here, poor mutt. Must be lonely." He gestured with the empty anesthetic gun at the length of benches.

"Oh, my God." Tears welled in her eyes.

Tier upon tier of cages in assorted sizes ran along the benches on both sides, the full length of the room. Rabbits, guinea pigs, hamsters, mice, and rats—and half a dozen cats of all colors.

"Cats are usually kept for neurological testing," Len said in a puzzled tone. "Don't know what they're doing in a cosmetics lab."

Her heart felt like it was shrinking. She wiped her eyes. "It's a bit academic, isn't it? They shouldn't be performing tests on animals for cosmetics at all. That's the law."

He snorted loudly. "Sure, the ban's been in place here for over a dozen years but if they can flout it for their benefit—and profit—then they'll try, won't they? People break the law all the time—and don't expect to get caught."

"Like us now, I suppose." She shrugged. "You're right, of course."

"Maybe they're testing for wrinkle treatment—botulinum toxin."

"Botox?"

"Yes. It's exempt from the ban, as it happens."

"Oh, my God. Really?"

She scanned the room. At the far end was a computer workstation and on an adjacent desk a laptop, its lid raised.

He put the dart gun in his bag and pulled out a video camera, started panning left and right, careful not to get Cat in the frame.

"This is just what I need," she said and pulled out her Olympus camera and moved about, taking a series of digital photographs.

Then she stopped in front of the rabbit cages. "They're all albinos!"

"They seem the best subjects, or so they say. More sensitive, I guess." He pointed to the laptop's screen. It showed columns of typed notes and figures. "These are Draize test results, see? It's a test on their eyes and skin, monitoring any toxicity and irritation—and the animals do get the odd side-effects, depending on the test substances."

She photographed the screen image, pleased to note the Ananke heading and the dates alongside tabulated results. "What kind of side-effects?"

"Ulceration, hemorrhaging, blindness," Len replied. "They're killed after the test."

Cat shuddered and ran a finger over her lips. She hadn't put on lipstick for tonight, obviously. She wondered if she'd ever want to wear the stuff again, then mentally shook herself. There were plenty of cruelty-free brands she could use.

She moved to the caged mice and took more pictures. "Cute, aren't they?"

"They're used because mice share a high percentage of genes with us humans. Tough luck on them, eh?"

"Poor things."

He gave a half-hearted shrug. "They could have ended up in a legal lab—for medical or warfare testing."

"Considering your feelings, I'm surprised you're so sanguine about this."

His features turned grim. "Virtually all our medicines and the lotions we use are as a result of pre-ban animal testing. It's a complex subject, tainted by the unethical people who work here and the rabid activists who threaten legitimate researchers with maiming and death."

Yes, complex, she thought. All about unnecessary suffering and pain. "I've got enough, I think." She capped the camera and put it in her bag.

"Let's go, then."

At the door, she paused. "What about the animals?"

"We leave them here. I'm not doing this to trash private property or release animals that'll end up being run over by a truck an hour later."

"All right." Before they'd set out, Len had ranted on about the extreme activists who seemed quite demented. Digging up a woman's corpse from a grave was not only quite horrible, it was insane he'd said. He had no wish to intimidate researchers or attract the attention of the National Crime Agency.

They retraced their steps to the kitchen area. He moved the chair aside and opened the door.

"Rain's stopped," he observed as they emerged from the doorway.

They hurried through the gap in the fence and reached the van without incident.

Finally, as they were driving off, Cat pressed her palms to her eyes. "I'm glad that's over."

"Took a risk but I think it'll be worth it. When're you meeting your journo contact?"

She glanced at the dash clock. "In an hour."

"Time for a beer?"

"Yes, I think I have." Her throat was dry and needed that kind of lubrication.

Len laughed. "Corks will be popping when our pal gets those photos published!"

"I imagine some people won't be celebrating," she said.

London

"Loup, what can I do for you?" Rick rose from his wide walnut desk as his boss entered his seventeenth-floor office. He glimpsed his secretary Mandy in the outer office, distress on her normally cherubic dimpled face. *What's going on?* Then the door slammed shut.

The great man was, as ever, impeccably dressed, today in a gray worsted lightweight suit. He was certainly not in a good mood. Loup scowled. He carried a tabloid newspaper, rustling it vigorously, and stormed across the fawn-colored carpet. He flung the paper onto Rick's desk. "What do you make of that?"

Rick stared, quickly scanning the double-page spread. He felt color drain from his face. "I thought you didn't have any animal labs in the UK."

"I don't tell you everything, Rick. Only what you need to know."

"So it seems."

"They've even put film of the raid on You-tube!" Loup slammed a fist on the paper. "How did this happen?"

Rick cleared his throat and rolled his eyes. "Animal Rights activists broke in. Seems like they incapacitated the power supply first. A pity—the CCTV might have been useful to the police."

"I have no wish to involve the police."

"They're going to be asking questions, surely?"

"Perhaps. I'm tempted to sue the hell out of the newspaper!"

"That might not be a good idea. You know how people feel about animal cruelty."

"They're lab animals. They have a good life..."

"...albeit a short one?"

Not amused, Loup scowled. "Enough of this. I've sacked Grayson, the director of the establishment, so they'll be hard-pressed to get much information. He kept everything close to his chest, by all accounts."

"Wasn't he following your company guidelines, then?"

Loup shook his head. "I understand that he strayed, thought he could get away with it. He won't work in this business ever again."

"He won't take the blame, then?"

"No, he won't. That's not a good idea. I'll explain Grayson was rogue and I dealt with him summarily. If this ever went to court, they'd like that. Swift justice, so to speak."

"Still, I suppose you will be facing a court case, a fine... What do your legal eagles say?"

Loup balled his hands into fists. "They advise I should appear contrite, apologize, and close the operation."

"Good advice." Rick gestured at the newspaper. "It'll all die down. In a week, it'll be forgotten. Yesterday's news"

"I suspect not."

"What makes you say that?"

Loup pulled out two photographs from his inside jacket pocket. "I think Ananke may be targeted by this person." He flung the photos onto the desk. They slithered over the newspaper and Rick leaned forward and picked them up.

"There was a laptop in the lab, and it was running on its own battery," Loup said. "It's used as a backup system and has a remote webcam to monitor the animals. These stills were captured from that."

Cathy Gledhill stared unknowingly from the photos.

"Isn't she your model girlfriend?" Loup asked.

Chapter 3

Bradbury & Hood

On his way back to his office, Loup frowned. The first time he'd encountered the Gledhill woman, he'd been positive they'd met before. And yet now, after seeing the web-cam footage and photos, he wasn't so sure, after all. Her features, the angle of her head—especially in the glaring lab light— his heart had threatened to erupt from his chest for a startling instant. No, she couldn't be... No, he had to be certain. Until then, he wouldn't act, tempting though it was to give the little bitch what she deserved.

As he opened the door of the ante-office, he started at the sight of Emilio Zabala waiting for him.

Zabala grinned and unfolded his wiry frame from a chair behind a low coffee table strewn with magazines.

Malorie, Loup's tall sylphlike brunette secretary said, apologetically, "Senor Zabala insisted he wait for you, sir, even though he has no appointment."

"That's all right, Malorie. I'll see him now—please rearrange my appointments. Give me half an hour, will you."

She reached for her phone. "Right away, sir."

Loup opened his office door and ushered Zabala in.

Loup crossed the fitted carpet and sat behind his desk.

In a loping walk, almost catlike, Zabala moved to the chair opposite and sat without being asked.

"I presume you were successful?" Loup queried.

Zabala's thin lips curved.

On reflection, Loup thought, that was a stupid question.

Southampton Old Cemetery

It was dusk, which made Detective Inspector Alan Pointer feel quite comfortable. He knelt on one knee by the body that slumped against a headstone, one of several in memory of forty-five Titanic dead. Not that there had been any bodies to bury, poor blighters, he thought. At least this corpse would eventually get a proper funeral: a middle-aged man, almost white hair, smart business suit, manicured fingernails, and long fingers, all broken. The wrists were slashed, and a kitchen knife and a bottle of pills lay in the grass by his side. Pointer glanced up at Detective Inspector Jardine of the Southampton constabulary; he hadn't come far. The central police station was a short distance down the road from here. Perhaps it was just as well, as Pointer doubted if the local DI could manage far, judging by his portly frame.

"Strange place to find him, isn't it?" Pointer said.

"It is." Jardine gestured at the male dog walker, who

hovered a few yards off beside a constable and Pointer's stout blonde bag-lady, Detective Sergeant Carol Basset, who was making notes. "It was by chance. The poor sod took a short cut."

"I find that short cuts can be the death of people."

Jardine grimaced. "That's been my experience too. Though, lately, we've had very few attacks on the Common. Local knowledge tells me this is no longer a regular haunt for muggers."

"This isn't a mugging. It's meant to be a suicide. But clearly it isn't, is it?"

"No." Jardine shifted his feet. "Obviously it was staged."

"Clumsily, though."

"I agree. How on earth could he slit his wrists if all his fingers were broken?"

Basset approached and, arms akimbo, and arched a blonde eyebrow. "Punishment, perhaps?"

"Precisely, Sergeant. Whoever did this made him pay for a transgression before sending him to join the rest lying in this somber place."

"Gives me the shivers, being here." And she fit her movements to her words while slipping her notebook into her bag. Her thin lips curled in distaste. "When my time comes, I want to burn."

"Cremation's not the same, is it?" Pointer stood and gestured at the higgledy-piggledy tombstones. "We're standing among stories of lives lived. It's quite a collection you've got here, Inspector Jardine."

"It is. Edwin Moon, a 1920 airman, war graves, Belgian servicemen, and even a chap who was a friend of Shaka Zulu."

"United Nations?" hazarded Basset, her wide hazel eyes glinting in amusement.

"United in death," Pointer countered as he turned to Jardine. "Thanks for alerting us. It was fortunate we were in the area."

Jardine shrugged and his jowls wobbled. "The deceased carried his ID. Worked for a corporation called Ananke. Our computers flagged that NCA is interested in anything to do with Ananke Corporation. Your cellphone number came up."

"I'm pleased the system works," Pointer said. He nodded at the corpse. "So, who is the victim?"

"Name's Richard Grayson," Jardine said. "He was the director of Ananke Outlet 5 until he got shafted."

Basset's eyes lanced the DI. "The lab that's been in the news, in fact," she stated.

"Yes. The same. But you both knew that since the news story is why you're here, isn't it?"

Tapping the side of his nose, Pointer's pallid lips smiled. "You're right but please keep it quiet. Ananke has been flagged for a while now. We're still building a case. It takes time."

He could see that Jardine was anxious to ask what kind of a case but, being the professional, he refrained. Instead, Jardine asked, "So, is this murder my case, or yours?"

"Oh, it's yours. Though I imagine it will be taken over by HMIT?"

Sergeant Basset looked askance at him. He mouthed *HMIT, the Hampshire Major Investigation Team.*

"Yes," Jardine replied, "we'll set up yet another murder incident room, naturally."

Pointer cocked an eyebrow. "Another murder? You're working on more than one fresh corpse?"

"Yes," Jardine said, "though this one's nothing like the other. Probably occurred near enough the same time as poor Mr. Grayson's..."

"Really?" Basset prompted, delving into her bag and producing her notebook again.

Jardine shook his head. "Not related, Sergeant. The other murder was a young woman. Found in a two-star hotel room. She'd been cut open then washed clean under the shower... The hotel reception staff isn't too meticulous in keeping records of guests. So long as cash crosses their palms."

"But it's a one-off?" Pointer said.

Jardine's jowls quivered. "I bloody well hope so!"

"Well, I wish you luck with that." Pointer folded his arms. "Now, what are you going to tell Grayson's wife?"

"What would you like me to tell her?"

"For now, say it was suicide."

"I should lie?"

"Not quite. Remember, it's staged, and you're meant to think that's the case. So go along with it but warn her that you're not completely satisfied."

"I can do that—subject to HMIT compliance, of course."

"Of course. We'll pool our knowledge; that goes without saying. I'd be interested to see the postmortem report as soon as it's available."

"You'll have it." Jardine shook Pointer's hand.

Basset said, "At least it's unlikely that spooks are involved, since the late Richard Grayson isn't dealing in non-existent Iraqi weapons of mass destruction."

Jardine eyed her as if puzzled by her manner.

42

"Not particularly funny, Sergeant," Pointer berated her. Basset's wry comment referred to the ostensible suicide of Dr. David Kelly in 2003 that was reviewed again about three years ago.

Northumberland

June was an unpredictable month. Come to that, Cat corrected, any month in the UK was "changeable"! So, the shoot's team was fortunate that the sun shone this week. In the past, she'd seen Holy Island—Lindisfarne —in the rain and the sunshine and felt that its medieval mystery worked better in sunlight. Yes, there was a certain brooding majesty when the place was viewed through sleeting rain or sea-mist, but it didn't appeal. Not when she was modeling evening gowns and cock-tail dresses; now, if the shoot had been about swimsuits and bikinis, rain wouldn't have been too bad, she supposed, for the models. Not that the catalog owners would want the photographs.

This shoot was for an autumn and winter collection —all taupe, green and cream—for *Vogue*.

There were ominous clouds out at sea, but they stayed there and didn't obscure the sun, to the delight of their photographer, Darren Taylor.

Yet a cloud hovered over Cat. She couldn't put a date or time on when she'd first noticed that she was being followed but she was positive she had a stalker of some sort. The term "stalker" should have sent a chill through her and twisted her gut, but it didn't. In the relatively short time she'd been a model, she'd learned to handle them—most were infatuated men of all ages, men who had no life of their own so fantasized about sharing it with their target. Harmless, most of them. Most. She hadn't encountered anyone she couldn't cope with, fend off, or dismiss. As a last resort, she could always fall back on her taekwondo training. None of her fellow models had experienced any real problems, either. "An occupational hazard, Cathy," Mirabelle had said once. It left her feeling wary and uncomfortable when one of these men approached her but that soon passed when he was informed that he was wasting his time.

"If they're persistent, I knee them in the crotch," advised Mirabelle.

Cat kept quiet about her potential taekwondo responses learned from her black-belt friend Mark.

No, she felt that this was something other than the normal type of male groupie. It began with the familiar tingle between the shoulder blades, then the blood rushing to her ears but, when she turned, nobody was anywhere behind her. They didn't have to be, of course. There were plenty of vantage points from where they could watch her, study her. Paranoid, *moi?*

She couldn't be definite, but she felt sure that the acute feeling hadn't happened until two days ago. Nothing presented itself after her infiltration of Rick's safe. Nothing after the cocktail party. Blood flushed her cheeks. After they'd broken into Lab A of Outlet 5...? Could be. Were there cameras or an undetected watcher? If so, why hadn't Dante called in the police?

In a quiet moment, she phoned Len and voiced her concerns. "Don't worry and don't do anything rash. I've got some leave due. I'll pop along and see you. Where are you staying?"

"We're all being put up at Bamburgh—the Victoria Hotel."

"Yes, I know it. I've been around that neck of the woods before, usually in winter to bird watch at Budle Bay. I stay at Seahouses. Call me tomorrow and we can meet."

Cat was teamed up with a male model and two other females for the Holy Island shoot. As she preferred being freelance, she always hoped that she'd get on with her fellow models. This time, she found them a good crowd, professional and without any noticeable hang-ups; and no divas, thank God! Nataliya was from the Ukraine and had mastered her English from films and television; Rosaria was Colombian who spoke Spanish-accented, halting English; Paul was from Wigan and spoke with a posh accent. She had been approached with an exclusive contract to walk for a particular designer shortly after she became a model; it had been very tempting, as it would have meant launching her career and elevating her status in the fashion industry with guaranteed work on the world's best runways. But she would have sacrificed her autonomy which in turn would have diverted her from her crusade against Dante and his Ananke Corp.

Their day started early, at 3:00 am because Darren wanted to get images in the can during first light. The two stylists had to work on their hair and make-up before Darren was ready with the lighting and his beloved Hasselblad.

It was a far cry from last month's session for the Littlewoods catalog. That had been hectic but mostly in the studio, donning one garment after another, more or less production-line stuff. She preferred these outings, really—time for artistry as well as fashion.

They were ready in time. The views took her breath away as the sun rose behind Lindisfarne, the silhouette emphasizing the mound and ancient buildings. She then turned her back on the beauty and Darren posed her, arms akimbo, in the black bodice, multi-colored check skirt, with leather boots; judiciously reflected light from umbrellas and the beauty dish enhanced the material and prevented her from being a mere silhouette like the background.

During quiet moments, her thoughts returned to Rick. Did the means justify the end? She'd drugged him and felt nary a qualm about it afterward. Is this how Loup Dante built his empire? Shunning conscience. Self-vindication. This sort of introspection spooked her.

The day's session ended at 7:00 pm and they all repaired to the hotel, exhausted. Tomorrow, thankfully, she had the afternoon off. Nataliya and Paul were posing as couples for overcoats and rainwear; at least they didn't have such an early start as Darren was very satisfied with the mood of his first-light photographs.

"TIME OFF FOR GOOD BEHAVIOR," Cat called it. She phoned Len and arranged to meet him in Seahouses. She waved cheerio to the team and was soon turning her Hyundai i30 onto the B1340 coastal road, leaving behind the imposing Bamburgh Castle and out to sea the Farne Islands—some twenty small islands that serve as breeding grounds for seals and hundreds of birds, among them puffins, terns, ducks, and gulls. Before long, she felt sure that a car was following her. A white Volvo. Or was it more paranoia?

She passed countless low stone walls and many charming stone cottages. The day was gorgeous, a brightness filled the sky, beaming off the pale gray cloud wisps. On her right-hand side, there were hedgerows, rolling meadows, trees and bushes, typical English countryside, and, on the left, the North Sea. The traffic was light which was fortunate as there was little opportunity for overtaking in this narrow road.

She followed the road into the town of Seahouses. The vast majority of buildings were stone-built, tan, and attractive. She drove past Barter Books, a smaller adjunct to the famous bookshop in Alnwick, and a tattoo parlor then turned into The Harbour Inn parking lot and braked next to Len's Ford Transit van. The inn's white curved facade appeared to be modeled on art deco architecture. She got out and left the lot, crossed the junction, and hoofed it along Main Street, past a newsagent's, a newspaper office, and finally pushed open the door into the Seafarers, a fully licensed restaurant and café. There was a welcoming aroma of tea, coffee, and fresh bakery.

Len was waiting for her. He waved from a table halfway along the right-hand wall.

"Where are you staying?" she asked as she sat opposite him.

"The Old Ship Hotel, overlooking the harbor."

"So, why park at the pub and meet here? Don't tell me you're not keen on pub grub."

"I like the home-made carrot cake, so sue me." He chortled as the attractive waitress approached. She took their order—two coffees and two portions of carrot cake.

Cat persisted when the waitress had left, "Seriously?"

"No. I have my reasons... That was quick! Ah, here's our order."

He paid, saying it was his treat. He no longer quizzed her diet choice as a model; it was her business whether or not she ate cake.

While he sipped his coffee, Cat mentioned the Volvo.

"But can you be sure you were followed?" he asked, cutting into his cake.

"As sure as I can be." She glanced over her shoulder. "Even now, I've got this tingling sensation down my back..."

He let out a laugh. "That's called guilt. We all experience it when we spot a police car popping into our rear-view mirror, remember?"

"No, this seems more pronounced than that silliness." She drank the coffee, hardly tasting it. The cake excited her tongue, though.

"I was only trying to lighten your load, Cat."

"I didn't mean it like that." She rested a hand on his. "Sorry."

"No problem." He drank then wiped his mouth with the back of his hand. "Now, where shall we break into next?"

She gave him a mock scowl. "Don't joke, this is serious. I've only started my campaign against Ananke. I don't want some busybody snooping and spoiling it!"

He touched his forelock. "I'm suitably chastised."

"Sorry—again!" She stopped, leaned across, and

removed a couple of crumbs from his chin. "Maybe I'm not cut out for this."

Len chortled. "You? Miss Nerves-of-steel? Give me a break!"

"I've been lucky so far. And that Lab exposé wouldn't have been possible without your help." She shook her head. "I'm not a private detective. I don't really know how I can maintain pressure on Dante and his nasty people."

He finished his coffee, and this time used the paper serviette to wipe his mouth. He shoved his chair back and stood. "I might have the answer to that. Coming?"

Puzzled, she dabbed her lips with her serviette and joined him.

They left the café and walked a short way along the path and then Len stopped and said, "Ta-da!"

"Pardon?"

He gestured at a door, the top half glass marked with the legend, *Bradbury & Hood, Private Investigation (Estab. 1896)*. It was squeezed in between a beauty salon and a betting shop. "Let's go in?"

She chuckled. "So this is why you wanted to meet here?"

He winked. "Method in my madness?"

"Your madness I already know about..." She pushed the bell and the door buzzed and instantly opened. "Trusting, don't you think? No intercom to ask who we are?"

"You can lie over the intercom."

"True," she conceded. They entered a small vestibule with carpeted stairs directly ahead.

"Anyway," he added, shutting the door, "we're probably on CCTV."

Cat felt the blood drain from her face, and she turned at the foot of the stairs. "Maybe we should go back outside?"

"No, we've come this far. I'd have thought you'd be comfortable on camera, being a model."

"I don't like being watched without my permission. It smacks of voyeurism."

"You're in the wrong profession, then. Humor me. Let's see if we can hire a private eye to identify your stalker!"

"Oh, all right. No harm in trying, I suppose."

They went up, Len leading.

At the first landing, there were three strong-looking paneled doors. The central one also revealed the same legend as outside. Len pressed the button and an intercom voice said, "Who is calling, please?"

"Miss Cathy Gledhill and Mr. Len Plummer. On a private matter."

There was a lengthy pause. Cat was about to press the button again, but a response forestalled her: "Please come in." The door buzzed and opened.

They stepped inside and a woman in her late twenties strode up to them and, smiling, shut the door. She was about five-five, her long black hair curling at her shoulders. She was slightly overweight and hadn't made allowances, her black skirt tight across her hips and her colorful butterfly-design T-shirt a size too small, bulging at her waist and a buxom bust.

"Hi, there. I'm Avril Bradbury, one of the two directors of the firm. Welcome!" She shook their hands and ushered them to two chairs in front of a disordered desk. On the other side of the room was another desk, presently vacant though there was a name on a wooden paperweight: *Mr. J. Bradbury*. Cat wondered where Hood had gotten to.

Avril slid behind the desk, made a half-hearted attempt to straighten the assorted sheets of paper and photographs and then thrust them in a drawer. All that remained on the desk was a notepad and a copy of the local newspaper, the *Northumberland Gazette*. "How can I help you, Miss Gledhill, Mr. Plummer? By the way, we're one of the country's oldest private investigation agencies still operating." She glanced around at the Spartan place, the floor covered in dull green linoleum. There was a four-drawer filing cabinet but no evidence of a computer and printer. "Not that I know how much longer that will be the case..." She offered another smile, her light brown eyes glinting.

Cat beamed back, liking the woman. "I think I'm being followed."

"Yes, you are," Avril said.

Cat looked at Len, astonishment on his face; she was taken aback, too. "How can you be so sure?"

"A mysterious gentleman hired our firm to keep an eye on you." Avril frowned. "My brother Jason will get the lashing of my tongue when he reports in, you can be sure. He isn't supposed to get detected!"

"I think he needs a less distinctive car than a white Volvo," Len suggested.

"I've told him, but he won't listen..." Avril sighed in sisterly exasperation.

Cat leaned back in her chair and relaxed. "That's a relief."

Len raised an eyebrow.

She returned his look. "Nothing sinister, I mean."

Then Len pulled a face. "Depends on who the 'mysterious gentleman' is, don't you think?"

"Yes, of course." She eyed Avril. "I don't suppose you can tell me his name?"

"No, sorry. He did seem concerned for your safety, if that's of any consolation?"

"My safety?"

"Yes. Are you in any danger?" Avril gestured at the local newspaper. "It says you're modeling at Holy Island. Perhaps there's an over-zealous fan following you?"

"Not that I'm aware of." A sinking feeling hit her stomach. No, it couldn't be Ananke. They couldn't link her to the Outlet 5 break-in. Was it her relationship, if it could be termed that, with Rick? Did Ananke, as a matter of course, hire people to monitor anyone who came into contact with their company lawyers? Not that they'd have a lot of company lawyers. *Getting paranoid, Cat. Rein it in!*

Avril stood and rested her hands on her desk; there was no wedding ring, Cat noticed. "Well, professional ethics suggest I should ask you to leave now." She bit her lip. "I'll call off Justin and terminate our contract with...with our client."

Len bobbed his head at her then stood and loped to the door.

Still troubled by the reference to her safety, Cat slowly got to her feet. Absently, she held out her hand. "I'm sorry you've lost your client."

"Don't be. It's clear that Justin needs to find a new career." She let out a half-laugh. "And me, as well, probably. Sorry."

They shook hands.

Once outside, Len led Cat away from the entrance. "Do you believe her?" he asked.

"Yes, why not?"

"She didn't have to tell you they'd been hired to put surveillance on you. We wouldn't have been the wiser."

"But if we'd hired her, there'd have been a conflict of interests. Imagine both a husband and wife hiring the same agency to have each other followed! It would be laughable!"

"Ethically, it's out of order, I agree. But I didn't know private investigators were that ethical..."

"You can't believe everything you read in the press or see in the films, Len."

He chortled. "Yes, but how do you tell what is true and what isn't?"

"The news story about Outlet 5 was true, all of it, and they reported truthfully."

"This time, because it embarrassed someone."

"Touché." As they passed Cuthbertsons, the confectioner and stationer's shop, she stopped walking and stared at the newspaper in the front window of the *Northumberland Gazette* offices. The headline read: *Ananke Plastics Manufacturing Plant repels demonstrators for third time!* She grabbed it, scanned the article—continued on page 6—and turned the pages feverishly. "This is worse than I thought," she whispered, looking up. But Len wasn't there.

Then she noticed him inside, at the shop's counter, a hangdog expression on his face. He came out with a pack of Players cigarettes. "I thought we'd better pay for the paper."

"And I thought you'd given up smoking?"

"You bring out the worst in me." He shoved the

packet into his pocket. "What's happening at the Ananke plant, then?"

"Protesters say the company's discharging toxic chemicals into the North Sea."

"So, despite what you said about half an hour ago, you actually have targeted another Ananke operation, is that it?"

"Well, I knew the plant was here..."

"And this happened to fit in with your latest modeling assignment?"

"Sort of. Remember, Ananke is spread far and wide. They've got places all over England and Wales, for example."

"Scotland?"

"Not that I'm aware of, no."

"Sensible Scots." He looked sideways at her. "So, you must have an angle already, am I right?"

"Yes. I'd read on the Internet that the Ananke people weren't too popular with some of the locals..."

"Are we sure they're locals kicking up a fuss or are they rent-a-protest anarchists out to smash a few police heads and embarrass the capitalist establishment?"

"Nothing is simple these days, you know that, Len. Some twenty years ago, people might have gone in for group sex. Now it's group texting. Text and hey presto you have a protest."

"I missed out on the group sex thing...you must enlighten me some day."

She elbowed him and folded the newspaper. "Only information I got from research—actually that would be before my time! You know, I wonder if we could still hire Avril. I mean, there can't be too many enquiry agents in a town this size."

Len stroked his chin. "Maybe. It might depend on what you hired her for, eh?"

"We need the dirt on Ananke Plastics that's on her doorstep."

"And you think she'll be able to dig up that any time soon?"

"She's local, so she must keep her ear to the ground, her nose to the grindstone—and all those other clichés you love—just to stay in business."

He threw up his arms. "Okay. I give up. Let's try her—again."

Chapter 4

Cat's Tail

"It's interesting you should ask," Avril said, rising from her chair. "I've built up quite a dossier on Ananke Plastics." She opened the top drawer of a filing cabinet and pulled out a bulging manila folder. "A number of local activists have hired me from time to time to dig around. I'm quite familiar with the Ananke security staff now. They had a choice—be nice to me or face bad publicity. They opted for the former."

"You mean you can get inside?" Cat felt her pulse racing.

"Yes, by appointment, of course." She returned to her seat. "Mrs. Hannigan is the administrator—very efficient but friendly enough. She's supplied me with the latest statistics, discharge readings etc." She shook her head. "They're clean, as far as I can tell. I testified as much when they had an inquiry two years back."

"An inquiry?"

Avril nodded. "An investigative journalist—David Ambrose, I think his name was—broke into the plant

56

and had a fatal accident. The plant—and Ananke Corp —were exonerated. It was in all the papers at the time."

Two years ago. "But who's to say that the findings then are still applicable now?"

Avril pulled out a sheaf of papers. "They produce monthly reports. They're verified by the council's pollution expert."

"They have a pollution expert—a town this size?"

"No, the council's in Morpeth and that's merely one of the town surveyor, Brian Cragg's, titles. You know, these days councils invent any number of job titles to make them feel important, justify their high tax rates, that kind of thing?"

"Oh, yeah, I know," said Len, grinding his teeth.

"Do you still regularly go into the plant?" Cat asked.

"Yes," Avril said. "I get a small retainer from one of the anti-pollution groups, DOSE - Defenders of Sacred Earth. Not much. But they want me to continue just in case anything goes amiss. They keep quoting PCB pollution at me. I point out that the stuff's banned but they insist I carry on checking. Distrustful lot..." She shrugged. "But they pay."

Len tapped his fingers on the desk. "PCBs?"

"Polychlorinated Biphenyls," Cat said. "Highly toxic, used in the manufacturing processes of paints, adhesives, polish, electrical equipment. Firms were pretty cavalier with it..."

Len let out a light laugh. "Is this the chemist in you coming out now?"

"You're a chemist?" Avril said.

"Yes..."

Avril leaned forward, in interrogator's mode. "But I thought you were a model."

"I'm both. Modeling pays better—and my hours aren't so regular.'

Avril narrowed her eyes and faced Len. "Cathy's right. PCBs were banned in the late 1970s, early 80s."

"Well," Len said, "that's all right, then, surely?"

"No, not really," Avril replied.

Cat explained, "What Avril means is that PCBs can remain in seawater for a thousand years…"

"Oh." Len fidgeted. Cat guessed he wanted a cigarette all of a sudden. "I presume the reports you're getting are still all right—clean, as it were?"

Avril sat back and gave a crisp nod. "I'm almost part of the furniture as far as Ananke's concerned. If it wasn't for the retainer, I wouldn't bother. I could write their report for them—it's virtually identical every time. They've got a tight system of checks and balances; it was explained to me. They're well within the safety limits."

"Who's to say their readings are ever taken," Len posed, "or even real?"

Avril glanced at the desk.

He leaned forward, his forearms on his thighs. "You haven't seen them taking readings, logging the details, have you?"

"Well, no… I tried to insist but they threw so much health and safety crap at me, I gave up insisting."

Len squinted at Cat. "If they're worried about marine life and seawater pollution, wouldn't the protesters have tested the seawater beyond the plant? They don't have to be inside the plant to do that, surely?"

Cat nodded. "You'd think so... But it depends how Ananke discharges the processing waste. Where do the protesters make their tests? If Ananke has constructed a pipeline that goes well out to sea, unless the discharge area is obvious—the bloom of discolored sea, for example—then it's invisible."

Avril raised her eyebrows. "What are these blooms you mentioned?"

"A discoloration caused by microscopic organisms in the water. Sometimes it appears like scum on the surface—it's cloudy and can be easy to spot."

"Then," Avril mused, "DOSE haven't detected any or they'd have played merry hell."

Cat wasn't going to admit defeat, however. "Can you arrange a visit—and take us with you?"

"Why?"

"I'd like to look over the place, see if there's any evidence I could use against Ananke."

"You don't seem to like Ananke very much, do you?"

"No, I don't, Avril. Right now isn't the time to explain."

"You're not planning anything illegal, something that would harm anybody, are you?"

Cat shook her head. "No, if anyone's involved in illegal acts, it's Ananke. The Southampton incident is but one of many. You saw the national papers?"

"Yes," Avril said, "that was awful. Those poor animals! Their director was found dead, committed suicide, so the report says. If you ask me, that was too good for him."

Cat started but quickly evaded Avril's eyes. She'd missed that news item somehow; too involved with the photo shoot, probably. Suicide? That *was* convenient. *Too convenient.* The man couldn't answer any awkward questions now. She shrugged a shoulder, hoping to dislodge the growing paranoid chip from it.

Vauxhall, South London

Sergeant Basset left her bags by the office door and approached her boss's desk. "I can't find my bucket and spade, sir. Do we really need to go to Seahouses?"

"We won't have time for leisure, Sergeant. We're going because I'm suspicious." Pointer leaned back in his chair. He rubbed a big hand over his drawn features and then studied her with those penetrating dark brown eyes. "The Grayson 'suicide' makes me wonder about the 'accident' at their plant."

"I've read the reports, sir. The inquiry seemed thorough."

He locked his desk drawer, pocketed the keys, and stood. "Stop playing devil's advocate, Sergeant. We're going and that's final." She followed his gaze out the window. The sky was deep blue only blemished by a few wisps of cumulus nimbus. "We'll travel when it's dark, of course..."

"Of course, sir. I know: when the sun's gone down." Not for nothing was he called DI Mushroom behind his back, she thought. She'd been with him on that case in Devon and knew the truth but he was reluctant to talk about it, even to her. So the rumors abounded to explain why he was reluctant to venture outside in daylight and she couldn't counter them on account of her promise never to speak of it. Naturally, there'd been conjecture that he was a vampire which was ludicrous; fortunately, the epithet DI Dracula hadn't stuck though Mushroom had. After the incident, he'd been hospitalized for weeks then only returned to work a month or so afterward. Her heart went out to him. A widower, he was pathetically grateful that he was kept on, despite his peculiar working limitations. "I've got a car waiting, sir, when you're ready."

"Good." He turned to face her, his pallid lips approximating a smile. "And thanks. I certainly wouldn't want to travel by train."

"I know, sir. We can go at our own pace this way. It's a full moon so it should be a pleasant night's drive."

Seahouses

Avril drove her red Vauxhall Vectra on the B1340 road toward Beadnell. She hadn't changed her clothing even though it was a new day; she still wore her butterfly T-shirt and tight skirt, which rode up her thighs, Cat noted, sitting beside her. In the back, Len seemed to be having difficulty keeping his attention out the window.

It was a warm day. The flat expanse of fields on both sides was dotted with sheep, a good number of them black. They passed a little traffic and a single-deck bus destined for Alnwick. A couple of miles south of Seahouses, Avril turned off and drove along an approach road that headed toward the sea. Halfway along, they passed a blue sign that stated *Ananke Biodegradable Plastics*. The complex was visible before they got to the entrance. It comprised of a number of two-story brick buildings and, behind these, a brick chimney and long single-story buildings. Huge metal pipes, many on gantries, seemed to snake every-where. Vans and trucks blazoned with *Ananke—Your Future Now* were parked over on the right, near loading bays.

Avril pulled up at the red-and-white striped vehicle barrier.

A dark-haired man in a blue uniform exited the gatehouse with a clipboard under his arm.

Lowering the window, Avril leaned on the sill. "Hi, Jerry, nice to see you again."

Jerry the security man leaned toward her, his eyes on her exposed thighs. "And you, Miss Bradbury. Pleasant surprise to see you so soon." He leered. "Your next monthly visit isn't due for a couple of weeks, is it?"

"That's right. This is a special one." She thumbed at Cat and then Len. "Two reps, Gledhill and Plummer, who want to meet Mrs. Hannigan."

His eyes ranged over Cat appreciatively, though he couldn't see much as she had her briefcase on her knees, and he hardly glanced at Len. "Yes, of course. She phoned, warned me to expect you all." He handed a clipboard through Avril's window; fixed to it were three laminated badges and safety pins. "Sign for the badges here, please."

Cat and Len signed and detached their badges, then made a great play of fixing them to their lapels. Cat had decided to dress down and wore an M&S fawn suit comprising of jacket, skirt, and a mauve Deben-hams blouse. She'd tied her hair up with a mauve ribbon that dangled at the nape of her neck. Len had made an effort and wore stone-washed denim jeans and jacket and a black T-shirt.

"This is probably my last visit," Avril said.

"Oh," Jerry said lifting his gaze to her face, "sorry to hear that."

"Thanks for everything, Jerry."

"No problem, Miss." He retrieved the clipboard from her, backed off, and pressed a button on the box at the end of the security barrier.

The barrier slowly raised, and Avril drove through.

"That was easy enough," Cat said.

AVRIL CLOSED the outer door behind them as Mrs. Hannigan stood, walked around her desk, and held out her hand. "Pleased to meet you, Miss Gledhill, Mr. Plummer." She was perhaps in her early fifties, Cat reckoned. Smart, in a light dark green pleated skirt and a white open-necked blouse. A single string of white beads adorned her neck and matched her earrings. Her hair was gray, almost white, and cut short. Behind her bifocals, her blue eyes appraised Cat and Len. She seemed a "no nonsense" kind of woman who took her responsible position seriously.

"It's good of you to see us at such short notice." Cat clutched her briefcase under her arm and shook hands, offering a genuine smile. She had no axe to grind with the Ananke staff, necessarily, only with the firm's head.

"Likewise," said Len.

It was a standard utilitarian office, a faint hum of air-conditioning barely discernible. Two other doors led off to the right. Behind Mrs. Hannigan's desk was a small wall-mounted key-safe, its door open; three bunches of keys were on hooks inside. Cat noticed a fourth set dangling from the filing cabinet's lock at the top right corner.

Avril said, "Contrary to recent media releases—and protests—the Activist Group is very satisfied with the reports you've been providing. They're consistent. Their fears seem groundless."

Mrs. Hannigan beamed. "I'm sure Mr. Dante and the board will be glad to hear it."

"But..."

"But?"

"Would it be possible for us to have a final reading and watch while it was taken?"

Pursing her lips in thought, Mrs. Hannigan went to her filing cabinet. She opened the second drawer, leafed through a file and pulled out a folder. "But Avril, the last report was only two weeks ago..."

"I know but they feel that if they showed everyone how the readings were taken, it would satisfy the few hot heads. Defuse them..."

Cat was impressed by Avril's certitude. She has me half-convinced already, she thought.

"It's rather unorthodox," Mrs. Hannigan mused, and her brow furrowed. "Still, if it would mean an end to all that...nonsense..." She closed the folder and replaced it in the cabinet drawer. "Very well. I'll have to phone George and arrange for him to take the readings of the effluent." She pulled a face. "He'll probably insist on everyone wearing hard hats."

"I know, health and safety," chimed in Cat.

"Quite. Sometimes, they go overboard. Still, we have to toe the line or risk facing a fine."

"Lawyers!" Len said with feeling.

"We must keep the lawyers happy!" Cat added, fleetingly thinking of Rick.

Mrs. Hannigan went to her desk, moved aside the open desk diary, lifted her phone, and dialed. "George, it's—yes, it's me. I have an unusual request to make..." She explained, nodded, smiled, and then hung up. She turned to Cat. "George is happy to oblige. 'Just this once', he said."

"That's good of him," Cat enthused.

"It certainly is," added Len.

Mrs. Hannigan went over to the filing cabinet and withdrew the keys and pressed home the lock. Then she opened her desk drawer and flung the keys in, shutting it.

It wasn't just health and safety that Mrs. Hannigan had no time for; basic security was not her strong point, either. Cat thought that this might be an opportunity worth grasping, rather than casing the place for a subsequent risky break-in.

"Follow me," urged Mrs. Hannigan. She led them to the far door, opened it, and they walked along the corridor.

After a few paces, Cat stopped and raised the back of her hand against her forehead. "Sorry, Mrs. Hannigan..." She indicated the door to the ladies' WC. "I fear morning sickness is about to discommode me..."

Turning, Mrs. Hannigan was solicitous. "Oh, dear. Shall we go back to my office, wait...?"

Cat waved her away and smiled weakly. "No, I'm almost used to it. I'm sure it will pass in a moment. I'll catch you up..."

"Very well. When you're ready, follow this corridor...around that corner...on to the end. There's another door with our security man on it. Tell him who you are; I'll warn him to expect you."

"I've got it, thank you."

"George will be waiting for us," Mrs. Hannigan said. "Are you sure you'll be all right?"

"Yes, thanks. I'll catch you up." Feeling a little guilty at the deceit, Cat left them, crossed over, pushed the ladies' door, and stepped inside. Catching her breath on the excessive smell of disinfectant, she leaned her back against the door. Nobody occupied any cubicles. She hoped Len would be able to play it by ear; Avril had certainly managed it very well up to now.

She waited about five minutes, opened the door a crack, and peered out.

They'd gone around that corner.

Cat retraced her steps to Mrs. Hannigan's door and entered her office.

If I'm going to be doing much more of this, she reasoned, I need to find an expert who can teach me how to crack a safe and pick a lock!

She opened the desk drawer, picked up the bunch of keys, and unlocked the filing cabinet.

The reports file was askew and not replaced smoothly. This allowed her to notice the folder behind it. The heading told all: *Alternative reports. On no account are these to be divulged outside Ananke.* Oh, God, this is gold dust!

She shoved the reports into her briefcase and snatched a blank A4 notepad and replaced the reports in the folder with the pad. Her heartbeat had increased as she put the keys back in the drawer. She snapped the briefcase locks shut as the outer door was opening.

Hastily, she dumped the briefcase on top of the filing cabinet and turned to the dark-haired newcomer who entered.

"Can I help you?" she asked, surprised that her voice sounded almost normal. Maybe a little hoarse and dry to her ears.

"You're new, aren't you?" It was a harmless question, yet his accented voice seemed tinged with menace. His dark, almost black eyes leveled on hers. He was of Latin descent, possibly South American or Spanish. She was surprised to see he carried a bulging dark leather Filofax.

"Yes," she replied, "I'm an intern, learning the ropes with Mrs. Hannigan. She's just popped out." That sounded convincing, she felt sure. "Can I help you—or do you want to come back?"

He produced a business card from his Filofax. "I visit at quite irregular intervals. She isn't expecting me. I work under Mr. Dante."

Sweat pooled at the waistband at her spine. Her hand was quite steady as she took his card. *Emilio Zabala. Head of security* the card informed her.

That was a Basque name. So...Spanish. She wondered if he knew that in Arabic his name meant "fertilize with manure". She said, "I'll let her know you called..." Still holding the card, she leafed through the desk diary. "Do you want to make an appointment?"

"No. The nature of my work suggests, how shall I say, that I arrive unannounced. That always brings more...better results."

"Yes, I'm sure it does."

He pointed to the wall key safe. "For example, I think it best if that safe was closed properly, don't you?"

She turned. Her face flushed warmly. "Yes, of course. An oversight. We normally..."

"Don't explain." She noticed him study her hand as she shut the safe and twirled the combination wheel. "Laziness in security can lead to serious breaches. Remember that, Miss..."

Not much evaded his eye, she realized. He'd clearly noted no wedding ring. "Golightly," she said. "Emma Golightly." Where the hell did that name spring from? Jane Austen having a *Breakfast at Tiffany's*?

"Enchanted, Miss Golightly."

She went across to the filing cabinet and thumbed the lock shut.

His lips curved. "I hope we shall meet again."

"That would be nice, Mr. Zabala," she responded lamely, tapping his card with a fingernail.

As soon as he left, she threw his card on the desk, grabbed her briefcase, and raced to the door she'd last entered. She opened it and checked the corridor. Nobody about. She let out a huge breath. Her hand felt clammy on the briefcase handle. She wiped her palm on her skirt.

Walking at a fast pace, she rounded the corner and soon reached the door and the security man. The climate control hadn't cooled her.

"Miss Gledhill, I've been waiting for you." He opened the door and then pointed along the corridor. "Take the second corridor on the right, keep going for about ten yards and you'll come to a door marked 'Plant'. I think Mrs. Hannigan will be waiting for you there with George—that's where you'll be issued with your overall and hat."

"Thank you. Much appreciated."

RESTING a hand on the steering wheel of his blue Renault Fluence, Emilio Zabala lifted his Filofax from the passenger seat and his lips curved at a memory. Petra frequently berated him for not using an iPod or tablet but, twisting her arm painfully and kissing her, he dismissed her comments airily, "I prefer paper—it's easier to dispose of." Now, he opened it, exposing a double page showing the week's diary. He'd remembered correctly; he'd scrawled Barmouth in tomorrow's section, a telephone number and alongside this, *time?*

He dialed the number.

A gruff voice answered, "Yes?"

"Hello, who am I speaking to?"

"Jenkins. What's it to you? Who are you, anyway?"

"This is Señor Zabala. I am ringing to confirm I will be there at 3:00 pm tomorrow. Is that convenient?"

"You can come any time you like, mate. We're ready."

"That is good to hear, Mr. Jenkins." He closed the call. That meant he had ample opportunity to dally here a little longer. He speed-dialed a number from his phone's address book.

When Loup Dante answered, Zabala said, "Do you employ interns at your Seahouses plant?" No need for introductions, Dante's phone would show the caller's name.

"Of course not. They may be cheap labor, but they've got no loyalty."

Yes! Something about the Golightly woman hadn't rung true; the visitor badge she wore?

Dante broke into his thoughts. "Why do you ask?"

"Oh, something cropped up in conversation during my visit. I'll keep you informed."

"Yes, do, I'd like—"

Zabala closed his cellphone and watched the other vehicles in the parking lot.

BY THE TIME Cat got to the door, she was sweating heavily. Not much got by Mrs. Hannigan, either. "Are you sure you want to continue?"

The incriminating folder in her briefcase seemed to weigh heavier by the minute. This may be an appropriate time to back out. Her encounter with that security man, Zabala, had shaken her. Something about his cold manner, his eyes. She wanted to be away from the premises before it was discovered that the alternative report folder was missing.

Len looked at her, his eyes reflecting confusion, while Avril's showed concern.

Cat brushed a hand across her forehead and hoped she wasn't overdoing the dramatics. It came away damp with sweat, which was genuine enough. "I think you're right. I'd better go back to the car... Len, Avril, can we do this some other time?"

"Yes, of course," Avril said, her eyes reflecting puzzlement. "It's a shame, though, if we could have drawn a line under what's happened and observed these readings being taken—"

"Do you want to go with me, Avril?" Mrs. Hannigan asked, eyeing her and Len.

Maybe he wasn't psychic, but Len detected something was amiss. "No, thanks. Avril, I know it's a shame, as you say, but let's take a rain check, eh? Cat needs rest —and you're the driver, I'm afraid." He shrugged.

They made their way back to the office which was empty.

Avril took the lead: "Thank you for being so helpful and understanding."

They shook hands and Mrs. Hannigan escorted them to the entrance and then left them.

As they descended the steps, Len whispered, "What's wrong?"

"I've got the alternative reports in my briefcase," Cat said. "We don't need to take any more readings—"

"Alternative?" Avril breathed, "My God, the bastards!"

Len let out a whoop of laughter and abruptly clamped a hand over his mouth.

Cat pointed to Avril's parked car. "Let's get away before Mrs. Hannigan realizes there's only a blank writing pad in her folder..."

"Bloody hell, Cathy!" Len whispered hoarsely.

Avril's key fob beeped. They opened the car doors and clambered in.

"Remember," Cat warned, hugging her briefcase, "we're not clear till we're through the barrier!"

"I'm not sure where this leaves me, actually," Avril said, starting the car. "I introduced you and when they discover the theft—make no mistake, that's what it is— I'll be considered an accomplice, an accessory."

"I know, I thought about it," Cat said. "The ethics of what I'm doing are never far from my mind, I assure you. But I can't see how they could make any charges stick once it's revealed they've been keeping a second set of reports. It's like double book-keeping in accounts.

Probably something similar goes on with the climate change zealots—anything to hide the true figures."

"You know, that doesn't make me feel any better." Avril scowled, her hands tight on the wheel as they approached the security barrier. "Couldn't you just stick to modeling?"

WATCHING Avril's red Vectra leave the parking lot and head for the barrier, Zabala dialed his cellphone.

Mrs. Hannigan answered almost at once.

"Ah," he said, injecting concern in his voice, "glad I caught you."

"I'm sorry I missed you, Señor Zabala. I found your card on my desk."

"Yes, I dropped in on the off-chance..."

"How can I help, Señor?"

"Please check to see if anything is missing from your office."

"Now? You mean, right now?"

"If you would; perhaps the filing cabinet or your drawers... I'll hold."

He waited two minutes and thirty seconds.

Her end rustled and then she gasped. "A—a—there's a report, it's missing... It must've been—"

He sensed his pulse rate increase. "Phone the gate-house, see if we can block them there. I'll follow them, in case they've already gone through."

CAT STOPPED PHOTOGRAPHING sheets with her cellphone and raised her head as Avril said, "I hope you've got some good material in there."

"Yes, there's plenty. The readings are way beyond acceptable. I can't understand how they can get away with it—the regular sampling of the seawater would give them away...unless—"

"Well, I'm glad it's been worthwhile," Avril said grudgingly, "because I've got some bad news."

"What is it?"

"We're being followed." Avril thumbed at her wing mirror as their car turned a bend. "A blue car..."

"What?" Len exclaimed. "They can't have got onto you—us—so quickly!"

"I could be having a paranoid episode but that car behind us has been on our tail for the last fifteen minutes." Avril snapped, "Don't turn to look, Len, we don't want him to know he's been spotted!"

Cat heard the revs increase and hedgerows now passed at an alarming rate. "You're going to outrun him?"

"Let's see what he's made of," Avril replied. "I know these roads. But does he?"

Chapter 5

Cat's Fish

They lost their tail at a set of traffic lights.

Shortly afterward, Avril dropped them off at the Harbor Inn parking lot, near Len's van. "Don't call me anytime soon, Cathy Gledhill. I suspect I've got my work cut out concocting a plausible story to explain your theft!"

"Well, you said you might have to change occupation," Len quipped.

"That isn't in the least amusing!" Avril stormed.

Len spread his arms. "We're the good guys, remember?"

"That doesn't help, Len."

Len offered an apologetic smile and Cat leaned on the car's sill. "Thanks, Avril—and we're sorry we compromised you."

Avril wafted a hand across her flushed face. "You had my adrenaline going for a while back there, the pair of you. I admit, it was exciting and beats the hell out of divorce cases! Don't worry, they can't prove anything."

"You're right," Cat said. "I checked the office; there were no security cameras in there."

Avril looked askance at her. "You know, if you ever want to pack in modeling, there might be an opening for you with us."

Cat grinned. "When my crusade against Dante is over, I might give it some serious thought!"

"Right. Justin isn't going to believe this!" Then Avril revved the engine and sped away.

Cat threw her briefcase to Len. "It's all yours—the sooner you get it to your journalist buddies, the better!"

"Where are you going?" he asked.

"My hotel. The shoot completes tomorrow. I need an early night!"

"Will you be okay?"

"Yes. We know my stalker was only Avril's brother."

Len glanced at the road junction; there were no white Volvos. "Yeah, of course." He opened the door, got in, reversed the van, and then sped out the exit.

She beeped her car-lock, opened the door, and slid in behind the steering wheel. Avril was right. The adrenaline rush during their getaway was only now draining from her, leaving her slightly deflated. No matter how familiar the sensation—and free-climbing supplied plenty of that—the climb-down from a high always caught her by surprise. She clipped on the seatbelt.

Before she could insert the key in the ignition, she heard a vehicle pull up behind hers. She glimpsed in the rear-view mirror; the damned fool was blocking her exit! And then her stomach somersaulted: it was a blue car.

The driver got out of the vehicle and her blood ran cold. It was the Spaniard—Zabala!

He walked up to her window and tapped on it with a knuckle.

She opened it a fraction. "Oh, hello, Señor Zabala."

"What a small world, meeting you here, Miss Golightly."

"Yes, isn't it?"

"It was mere chance, my spotting you standing by this car."

Chance, my eye! "Really?"

"Well, yes. Last time I saw you, you were in a different car—as a passenger." His dark gaze slid from her face to the passenger seat and then to the back seats. He frowned.

Her mouth went very dry. She felt queasy. *Pull yourself together, woman!* "Have you been following me?" Her tone was accusatory, as she intended.

"I chanced to see you leaving the Ananke parking lot in a hurry with your two friends. At least, I presume they were your friends?"

"No." She forced a smile. "Only business associates. We do car sharing from time to time. Saves on fuel."

"Oh, I see. How...inventive, is that the word?"

"No, economical is the word you're seeking, I believe. Now, I'm sorry to sound impatient, but could you please move your car? I want to reverse out and I'm in a hurry."

"Where is your briefcase?" He glanced around and his eyes narrowed. "And where are the others?"

"Others?"

"Your car sharers."

"They've gone." She was less fearful, more annoyed

now, and infused her words with exasperation, "Like me, they have other business to attend to."

"I'm sorry, Emma Golightly," he said, his tone quite menacing, "but I will not let you leave until you return the documents you stole from Mrs. Hannigan."

"What?"

He unbuttoned his jacket and peeled back the right side to reveal a shoulder holster and the grip of an automatic pistol. "I insist."

She swallowed and her legs felt incapable of even manipulating the pedals; not that she had anywhere to go. "You can't threaten—"

"I have—and I *will* do more than threat—"

Abruptly, there was a loud crash behind them.

Zabala swung around, carefully buttoning up his jacket. "*Madre de Dios!*"

Cat peered over her shoulder. A red car had collided with Zabala's vehicle. The driver switched off his engine and got out. My God, it was Rick!

She unbuckled her seatbelt, opened the door, and got out; she wanted to shout, "He's got a gun!" But then she remembered the snub-nosed revolver in Rick's safe. Maybe she should duck out of harm's way? This was absurd, guns in Seahouses, of all places! Then she recalled seeing in the national news the story of an awful man, Raoul Moat, who went on a killing spree about four years ago not far from this area. No, maybe it wasn't so far-fetched.

Rick stood next to his Toyota Avensis and waved his arms in a gesture of contrition. "I'm awfully sorry, old chap." He walked over to Zabala's car and leaned in the open window on the passenger side then pointed at the glove compartment. "My fault entirely! Can we exchange insurance details?"

Zabala paced around the cars and hastily examined the damage, which seemed minor on his car. "I haven't got time for this—*move your car out of the way*, and I'll go!"

"No sooner said than done," Rick said and returned to his car, switched on the engine, and reversed into an empty parking bay. As he got out, he waved to the departing Zabala but received no reciprocal sign.

He strode over to her. "Some people are decidedly ungracious, haven't you noticed that?"

"Yes..." The relief that washed over her seemed almost physical. She felt her body tingle. Before, on being confronted with a gun, she'd felt chilled, out of her depth. Now, she felt the opposite, a quite pleasant sensation.

Then it hit her. Coincidences were piling up— unbelievably. Zabala wasn't here by chance. His was the car following Avril's, she felt sure. Rick being here wasn't by chance, either.

He turned and eyed his car's dented fender and slightly buckled hood. "Don't suppose you could give me a lift to my hotel?"

"Of course." It was the least she could do. "Where are you staying?"

"The Victoria, Bamburgh."

"Really?" Yet another fluke? "That's a coincidence, so am I—with our crew and other models."

"Well, that is a coincidence. I phoned for a booking. I got lucky, they said, almost full—no wonder with your crowd being there."

"*My crowd* packs in tomorrow, weather permitting."

As Rick unlocked his car's trunk and lifted out his Samsonite suitcase, she asked, "What will you do about your car?"

He shut the trunk and locked the car. "I'll phone a garage, arrange for them to pick it up, get it towed away, repaired..."

"What will you do in the meantime, while you wait for it to get fixed?"

"I can hire a car. Insurance allows it."

"Lucky you. Mine doesn't."

"Yes, lucky me. I've got a company deal. One of the advantages of not being freelance."

"I prefer the freedom—as implied in the term." She opened her door, got in, and popped her car's trunk. "Get in, then."

He put his suitcase in the trunk, shut it, and then smoothly slid into the passenger side. He belted up and sat with his hands on his knees, looking ahead. She studied his profile. Her cheeks flushed as she recalled undressing him. "Your arrival was very timely, Rick. Señor Zabala was pestering me."

Abruptly, he turned to face her. "That was fortunate, then. Zabala, eh?"

"You must know him. He works for Ananke."

"I know. But how do you know?"

"I've seen his business card."

He frowned and turned away. She switched on the ignition, engaged the gear, reversed, and then drove out of the car lot. She felt sure he had a question on the tip of his tongue, but he kept silent.

She moved into fourth, the road ahead clear. "Come on," she said, keeping her eyes on the road, "you deliberately drove your car into his."

"Yes. I noticed you both seemed to be having heated words. He didn't look too pleased. I might even say he appeared quite threatening."

"That was timely, maybe even gallant of you. But what are you doing here, Rick? And don't tell me it's a coincidence again. I won't believe it."

He sighed. "Very well. I got a phone call from Avril Bradbury. She apologized, telling me you'd rumbled her brother."

"You! You're the 'mysterious gentleman'?"

He let out a laugh. "Is that what she called me?"

"Yes..."

"How quaint."

"What isn't quaint is why you wanted me followed. Was it to keep tabs on me, until you could turn up?"

"No, I was genuinely concerned for your safety. And it seems I was right to be anxious."

She shuddered. "You might be right, yes. I know Zabala carries a gun..."

"He does, does he?"

She bit her lip, had almost said, "So do you!" Instead, she settled for, "Surely you don't really think I'm in danger?"

"I do."

"Why?"

"Because Loup Dante recognized you during the raid on Outlet 5."

The car juddered as she lifted her foot off the accelerator in shock. Quickly, she changed down and regained control. She checked his face hastily; he kept his gaze out the windshield. She concentrated on the road again. "He was there?"

"No. There was a webcam, videoing you both. You

got video of the lab while Ananke got video of you taking pictures."

"I knew we should have kept our balaclavas on! You don't sound surprised to learn that I'm more than a model."

"I was, when Loup showed me. I've had time to adjust, since. You and your pal were careless."

"Oh, God. Then the police..."

"Won't be involved. Loup has asked me to keep an eye on you. That's all."

"That's all—after the damage we've caused his company?"

"Yes. He was most adamant. No police, no recriminations—for now."

"I'm not sure I like that 'for now' bit." She followed Links Road with the sea on their right. "You must be well in with him, if he trusts you..."

"I doubt if he trusts anyone. But he's happy to keep me on a loose leash."

"What will you report to him—after we've been to their plant here?"

"That depends on what you've done and what you've learned."

Bamburgh Castle loomed on their right now as she negotiated the bend into Front Street. "When does the third degree start?"

"I thought tonight—over dinner, since we're both in the same hotel."

"What about the other models, the photo-shoot team?"

He shook his head. "Sorry. I can't afford to pay for them as well—only you."

"Wouldn't your company pick up the tab?"

"Touché." He grinned. "But I only want your company, not theirs."

She turned off the street and braked outside the entrance of the attractive brownstone-built Victoria Hotel. Switching off the engine, she leaned on the steering wheel and looked at him. "All right. On the understanding that I'll be having an early night, as we have to start first thing tomorrow. It's our final shoot."

"An early night? Could we continue where we left off? Can't quite remember when, it's a complete blank..."

"No, Rick." She felt her cheeks glow warmly. "You won't get a blank check from me tonight. We can indulge in Q&A, if you like, but that's the only game in town for you and me... For now."

"For now," he echoed, a smile on his lips as if he liked the sound of that.

SHE HAD DECIDED on wearing something simple for the meal, a Jasper Conran green geometric flared dress and, apart from small pearl earrings, no jewelry. Rick was waiting for her at a small, round table as she entered the light and airy Bailey's bar. He stood, looking smart in a beautifully cut charcoal plain twill suit and deep blue open-necked shirt. He walked over and gave her a peck on the left cheek. "You look gorgeous," he whispered in her ear. "Guerlain Idylle, I think?"

A thrill ran through her. "Thank you. You're right, of course."

He escorted her to the restaurant entrance and the maître d led them to a table beneath a huge mirror.

The menu offered a broad choice at reasonable prices.

Rick chose pan-fried Toulouse sausage, French black pudding and egg for a starter, and Northumbrian steak and ale pie, mushy peas, mash and gravy for the main, adding, "I feel a glutton, knowing how models must starve themselves. But I've always been partial to this pie!"

"Don't believe everything you read," she said. "Not all models are stick-thin. Many of us enjoy our food, though in moderation when we're on a shoot. But you must have assumed that already."

He nodded.

Strangely, they'd never had this kind of conversion before; possibly because whenever they had dined together, she'd been frugal with her choice of meal. "I think I can risk an indulgence or two tonight, anyway," she said and selected Thai fish cakes for her starter, to be followed by seared sea bream, saffron mash, kale, king prawns, and pancetta.

"My usual preference is a red," he said, "but I can recommend their Santa Serena Sauvignon Blanc—it's ideal for the fish."

He was right, the wine was dry, as she liked it, and redolent of citrus.

For most of the first half of the meal, she talked about the shoot on Lindisfarne and praised the professionalism of Darren, the photographer. She had to admit that every time they went out she felt at ease talking to Rick and he always made a good listener. Unlike many men, he seemed less interested in himself and his accomplishments and seemed genuinely fascinated by her.

Halfway through the main course, Rick lay down his knife and fork, leaned back, and fingered the stem of his wine glass. The humorous slant to his lips vanished. "During my contretemps in that parking lot today, I glimpsed Zabala's Filofax lying open on the passenger seat."

"I know, Filofax...in this day and age!" Her words echoed her thoughts when she'd seen it earlier today. She sipped her wine.

"I'm sure they have their uses. Not everyone's wired into the digital age quite yet. I don't see paper books going the way of the dodo for some time, actually."

"You're right, of course. Even though I have an e-reader, I still have a number of treasured books..."

"We've discussed a few already, as I recall?"

"Yes." Indeed, they had, yet the title that remained with her was Patrick Suskind's *Perfume*; perhaps because they'd been talking about it that night when she seduced him, drugged him, and then stole his safe combination. She felt her cheeks glow warmly. "What did you glimpse in his Filofax?"

"An appointment at Barmouth."

"Where's that?"

"Wales. My family used to holiday there most summers."

"My father and I holidayed in Spain, when he could get time off..." She glanced away then blinked to dismiss the painful memories.

"The thing is, Cathy, I wasn't aware of any Ananke offices or business plant in Wales."

"Oh?" She shrugged, playing devil's advocate. "Perhaps Zabala has friends or family there?"

He dabbed his mouth with the serviette. "This is where it got interesting. I called up the account files on my tablet. There are two phone numbers for the company in Wales. While I was getting ready, I telephoned Dai Carew."

She wrinkled her brow.

He explained, "He's a contact in my little green book."

She wasn't about to tell him she'd photographed all the pages of that book. "And was Dai able to help?"

"Yes. He got back to me minutes before I came down to dinner. He obtained the address of both phone numbers. One was in Cardiff but the other was very close to Barmouth. Interestingly, he was able to give me a Google coordinate. It's just off the A494..."

"Interesting. Dai sounds like a useful contact to have."

RICK FINISHED his apple and berry crumble. The vanilla anglaise was fine but he preferred proper custard. He was pleased to see that Cathy, true to her word, had put away almost all of her lemon cheesecake. The bottle of wine was empty, resting upside down in its ice bucket.

"We'll have coffee in the bar," he told the waiter.

"Very good, sir. And will that be all?"

"Yes, thanks. Coffee and the check." He led Cat by her bare arm, pleased to touch her even if only slightly. He swallowed drily, fleetingly reflecting on the image of her in her bra and skirt and their lingering kisses on that most odd evening. Park that thought, he told himself. *Behave!*

They moved to a quiet corner in the bar. There were four other patrons, apparently enjoying an aperitif before going in to dinner.

Within minutes, the waiter brought their coffees, mints, and a small salver with the check. "Sign here, please."

"I'll pay now, if you don't mind," Rick offered.

"Certainly, sir."

Rick verified the bottom line, did a swift calculation, and withdrew his billfold, then pulled out three twenties and a ten. "Keep the change."

"Thank you, sir." The waiter swung around and left them.

Rick folded his billfold but before he could put it away, Cathy's hand restrained his. "Can I have a look?"

"What, this?" He flipped open the billfold and showed her the photograph.

"Yes. I couldn't help but notice—your wife and children?"

He smiled wryly, again recollecting the night that offered so much promise yet ended in a confusing blank. Of course, she must have searched his billfold and seen the photo before; that was doubtlessly when she found the slip of paper with the combination on it. There was no evidence that the contents of the safe had been tampered with, yet that night her perfume had filled the air around the safe.

"Why are you smiling?"

"Do you always jump to the wrong conclusions? Is that what your obsession with Ananke is about?"

He'd hit a nerve. She flushed and, briefly, her misty blue eyes flashed. She turned her head away, studied her coffee cup, and then lifted it to her kissable lips.

He broke the silence. "It's a photo of my sister, Holly Ambrose, and her two girls, Mary and Louise, actually."

"Oh." The tone of blush seemed to deepen on her high cheekbones. The effect was highly attractive.

"If I tell you more, will you tell me why you're obsessed with Ananke?"

She lowered her cup. "I wouldn't say I was obsessed..."

"Breaking into my office, searching my safe, taking part in a raid on Outlet 5, upsetting Señor Zabala...?"

"What do you mean, breaking into your office? I'm sure the security man on the door wouldn't have let me anywhere near..."

"You're right, he didn't. I asked him. How did you get in?"

"This is absolutely silly. Why would I want to break in?"

"You've never been in my office, Cathy—yet when I popped in by chance, I noticed your perfume in the air —near the safe." He tapped his nose. "As I said, I have the nose for it."

"But if you guessed I'd done that, why did you take me out to the party?"

"Because I genuinely like you. I believed you had your reasons." He grinned. "I'm still puzzled how you got in. I'm sure you got the combination from my billfold—I remember letting that fact slip out one evening."

"Very well. But you have no evidence." She studied

him and he found her steady gaze alluring. "I suppose you're not wired?"

"You've been watching too many movies. My enquiries tonight are on my behalf, nobody else's."

"Since you seem to have guessed so much, I'll admit that I climbed the building and got through your window."

He felt a fool with his mouth open. He shut it. *My God, she climbed the bloody building!*

"Yes, you're correct," she said, "I found the combination in your billfold, where you said you kept it."

"The blank episode?"

Again she flushed, an even deeper red. "I'm sorry. As you'd inadvertently suggested the means of opening your office safe, I felt I had no option but to obtain the combination —"

"You drugged me." His tone held no accusation; he was simply stating a fact.

"I did. My professional training comes in useful sometimes. I said I'm sorry."

"That's not very ethical, is it?"

Her eyes narrowed and the color in her cheeks was no longer embarrassment but in anger. "You work for Ananke," she seethed, "so don't talk to me about ethics!"

He raised his hands in mock surrender. "Whoa, there, I'm really on your side, you know."

"I don't understand. It's as if you're playing cat-and-mouse with me —"

"I don't think you've got that quite right. You're the cat, Cathy... Climbing buildings, drugging dupes, cat-burgling, sneaking into premises..."

"Your coffee's gone cold. Let's get down to what you want."

He was tempted to hold her hand but resisted. "I want the same as you, Cathy."

She shook her head repeatedly. "No, you don't." Moisture collected at the corners of her eyes.

"Do you want to talk about this somewhere else, more private?" His fingers tentatively rested on hers.

She recoiled from the touch and sat back in the seat. "I'd appreciate it if you didn't turn on the charm, Rick." Her glossy thin lips curved in the semblance of a smile. "It's quite devastating. I really don't know if I could resist it..."

He sat back, too. "I think you can." He raised a hand and rested it on his chest, over his heart, which seemed to be pumping rather fast. "I give you my word, no charm offensive. But, believe me, Cathy, we do need to talk in private. Your room or mine?"

Chapter 6

Catch Up

She decided on her room, as she felt she could be in control then, though all sorts of feverish feelings washed over her as they entered.

"You've got a splendid view of the castle from here," he observed, lowering himself to a two-seater settee at the window. The castle was floodlit, a golden glow against the dark blue night sky.

She brought the kettle out of the en suite bathroom and plugged it in. "The view's at a premium. We drew lots for it and, for a change, I won."

The kettle didn't take long to boil, and Cat made coffee; both preferred it black without sugar.

She sat on the other settee opposite him, a small oblong table between them.

"Now," she said, "tell me about your brother-in-law, David."

"How'd you know his name?"

"I joined up a dot or two. Go on, tell me."

"All right." He lowered his cup to the saucer. "Dave

90

Ambrose was Holly's husband, an investigative journalist. He was good at what he did. He checked his facts and kept his stories close to his chest until he was ready for them to break. Two years ago, he foolishly broke into the plant of Ananke Plastics, Seahouses. The security patrol found him next morning. He'd fallen to his death..."

"Mrs. Hannigan mentioned the incident and his name."

"Ah, I see, the dots...?"

"Yes," she replied. "There was an inquiry. Ananke was exonerated and the inquest declared it 'an accident'."

He nodded. "I'd believed that too...until Holly went through Dave's things..."

"What did she find?"

"That's the problem. She found nothing. Nothing to do with Ananke in his computer files. Nothing on paper. Yet he was so fastidious about his work."

"Hidden files?"

"No, when she told me what she hadn't found, I checked."

"And neither of you know why he would have broken into the plant?"

"We supposed he was investigating. I mean, there had been a minor surge of complaints when the plant first opened but that soon died down once Sebastian Dipple got involved."

"Dipple?" She blushed again. "Those lewd photographs in your safe..."

He grimaced. "Yes, that's him. One of four MPs at Morpeth. He's a dark horse, representing the Independent Green Party."

"And he was keen to have a plastics plant built at Seahouses?" she said incredulously.

"Very keen. Dragged up the area's history—all about lime kilns. A small inner harbor was built there in the 1790s, mainly for the local lime industry. A large block of lime kilns was built on the harbor-side. He says the biodegradable material can be formed into packing materials, it can be extruded, and it can be injection-molded in modified conventional machines. Different types of fillers can be used with the system such as wood flour, clay, wastepaper, or lime..."

"I've heard about lime," she said. "When it's layered with coal and burned, the result is quicklime—used for making lime mortar. It's good for neutralizing acid soils and lightening clay soils. In fact, it's a disinfectant, makes caustic soda and soap and even whitens sugar, in the right quantity, of course. Otherwise, it's dangerous stuff."

He looked askance at her as if puzzled by something she'd said, and then went on, "Well, their lucrative business shut in the late 1850s due to competition. So the place was quite neglected until they discovered tourism for the Farne Islands. Dipple believed it was an ideal opportunity to bring more prosperity to the area."

"How philanthropic of him," she said. "Didn't he see anything wrong in espousing the 'green' cause and advocating the building of a plastics processing plant?"

"Dipple's a chancer who cottoned onto the green cause but his heart's not in it. One of his passions is doing deals, making money. And he was well placed, too, though he has kept it quiet. Still, I've only recently learned that his wife is on the board of directors at Ananke. Through her, he has clout."

"So, she wouldn't be best pleased to see those photographs you have in your safe."

"That's one of his other passions."

"How did you come by them?"

"Hold on a minute, Cathy. It seems all one-way so far. How about you opening up to me about *your* obsession?"

"In a moment, I promise. Tell me about the lewd photographs?"

"'Lewd'—I love that word. Seems so old-fashioned."

"It's the way I was brought up."

"Well, your parents did a fine job..." He stopped.

She felt her eyes tear up, glanced away, and blinked.

He hurried on, "I acquired the photos by using Avril Bradbury. She and Jason cover extra marital affairs as well as commercial misconduct..."

"Avril took those photos?"

"No. She 'found' them in Dipple's *pied-à-terre*."

"Naughty Avril," she said. "Enterprising but naughty. And?"

She was surprised to observe that his cheeks reddened.

RICK STUDIED his hands in his lap, surprised at his reticence. "I blackmailed Dipple into getting me the job at Ananke. I worked hard over the next two years and built up a good reputation, getting to the point where I'm trusted by Loup."

"While really filing information for eventual disclosure?"

He sighed. "Yes...until you started to upset everything..."

Her brows knitted. "I'm sorry. I didn't mean to interfere with your plans."

"That's all right. You weren't to know. It's nice to hear someone say sorry without appending an 'if'..."

"Meaning?"

"People in positions of authority. Haven't you noticed? They apologize but it's worded so that they don't accept any opprobrium. 'I'm sorry if you're distressed by...etc....etc....'"

"Opprobrium. That sounds old-fashioned too."

"I used to read a dictionary when I was young."

"I read encyclopedias, actually."

"So, we have something in common, after all!"

"Oh, I think the biggest thing we have in common is our distaste for Ananke...and Loup Dante."

"Distaste? I had a feeling it was much stronger than that, Cathy."

"You're right, of course." She peeled her gaze from his; it was her turn to study her hands in her lap. Surprisingly strong hands, he thought, if she really did scale the outside of his office building. "My turn, I think."

"Only if you really want to," he conceded gallantly, though inwardly he cursed his good self, wanting very much to hear her story. He got up, went over to a chair by the dressing table and removed his jacket, put it on the chair back. Returning to his settee, he said, "Go on, Cathy. I'm listening."

"Wherever I go, Loup Dante dominates my thoughts. Like a pall of doom."

He thought she was being slightly melodramatic but refrained from commenting. "Go on."

"I studied Chemistry at Oxford. Papa was so proud of me."

"Ah, that explains your interest in the quicklime process?"

She nodded. "Sadly, he never got to see me graduate; almost five years ago, he was killed in a hit-and-run car —"

"I'm so sorry... When I mentioned your parents..."

"My turn to say, 'You weren't to know'. That threw me, to be honest. I was suddenly an orphan."

"Your mother had died earlier?"

"Yes. Our family's middle name should be Irony. Maman was an excellent chemist. Naturally, I wanted to emulate her. My father told me quite a lot after my mother died. Not all at once but piecemeal. I put it all together, eventually." She smiled weakly. "Joined the dots... Their relationship with Loup Dante went back to their university days, in fact."

CAT DIDN'T TELL Rick everything, just the bare bones. One day, she might divulge the full story for him; and the flesh on the bones was considerable:

The young constantly reinvent themselves and the world, rediscovering things their elders take for granted. Her parents—though, obviously, they weren't that then— probably knew that Oxford had been an exciting place for students for centuries but, it seemed that in the 1960s, everything was different. Out with the old, in with the new. Perhaps they took heart from Harold Wilson's words when he was leading the Opposition. They were certainly keen to be part of "the white heat of the scientific and technical revolution" he espoused and, to prove it, they found daily challenges in their respective chemistry courses.

Loup was Swiss, the only son of a wealthy family who owned a pharmaceutical firm. He joined the university in 1966 to read chemistry and immediately excelled. Unfortunately, he suffered some disfigurement in a chemical accident in the lab but that did not deter him. He was a good rugby player and swimmer, and, despite yellowed teeth and his disfigurement, he was both handsome and popular with both sexes. His fellow students were not averse to telling him that it was most unusual for him to link up with someone who joined the college two years after him yet, Daniel, the newcomer from France, was precocious in the extreme, bordering on genius.

Within months of beginning his course, Daniel had the entire chemistry faculty buzzing; he was bold, innovative, and not scared to trample on old theories. Both young men found that they had much in common and enjoyed the other's company.

Some friendships flicker and fade, like guttering candles, others tend to gain strength from adversity and last a lifetime, impervious to the inevitable battering life offered as if cut from a diamond. In those heady days, it seemed that Loup and Daniel would be friends forever.

There was no rivalry between the two young men. Loup accepted that he would never be as good a chemist as Daniel. He knew he could still be successful and carve out a future for himself in his family business. And there was no rivalry over girls, either, because there were plenty around only too willing to accompany them to the balls, dinners, and sports events.

Then, Deborah Gledhill Radley joined the university from Portsmouth, England, in 1969, and it seemed as if everything changed overnight. Many heads were turned by the attractive young woman with long auburn hair and piercing blue eyes. She was athletic and humorous, and—like Daniel—she was capable of grasping the most complex theories about chemical structures and reactions. Surprisingly, Deborah found few like minds in her own intake year and gravitated toward Daniel and Loup. It seemed totally natural that they should form a threesome. They spent many late nights discussing the latest discoveries and poring over that week's *New Scientist*. While Loup was good, and Daniel was excellent, Deborah was simply brilliant. Not one of them would fail. Failure was never admitted to their lexicon.

Inevitably, the chemistry of hormones and pheromones reacted on the threesome. Loup was older and appeared more mature, almost a father figure to Deborah, even though he was only three years her senior. He made the first move, and she was surprised and flattered. Deborah had not thought of either Daniel or Loup in that way before. But now, it was exciting and, since Daniel hadn't shown any interest in her sexually, she didn't feel she was disappointing him or likely to break up the friendship between all three.

Yet when Daniel found out, he was furious, though not with Deborah. He was annoyed with himself. He couldn't blame Loup, either. They were friends, after all. Everything stayed almost the same. But Daniel burned with jealousy.

As time passed, Deborah began noticing small things about Loup's behavior. He rarely displayed anger or displeasure, but she realized that he was a bad loser. He always wanted to excel which, in itself, was not unusual in the heady environment they inhabited. Less palatable, however, he took excessive pleasure from winning. When he was selected to spend his final year on a full-time project with a big pharmaceutical firm in Geneva, he actually crowed about it to Daniel: "They've virtually told me I can get a job with them when I graduate. They're interested in my work on fragrances linked to pheromones." Daniel was pleased for his friend. Deborah was uncomfortable as she had been seeing less and less of Loup lately, yet he never seemed to remark on her absence from his life; he was so fired up with his career prospects.

The two lovers had a fight before Loup left for Geneva. He wanted her to give up her studies and marry him and go with him to Switzerland. She refused. Loup then accused her of going behind his back with Daniel which she obviously denied as it was totally untrue. Before, she had glimpsed an occasional somber side to Loup but now he became very unsettling. When he stormed out, her first instinct was to go to see Daniel.

Over a bottle of Blue Nun, she poured out her hurt and mixed-up feelings for Loup. She still loved him, and yet...Daniel was supportive, sitting away from her at the dining table while she slouched, quite bereft, in the settee. He argued for Loup: "It's a big opportunity for him, Debs. He doesn't quite know how to handle it yet, that's all."

But Loup's advocate was fighting a losing battle

and, besides, his heart wasn't in it. The pair went their separate ways at the holidays and simply expected to see each other again for the new term. They kept in touch but, as the weeks passed and Loup didn't make contact with Deborah, she despaired and telephoned Daniel. They met on neutral ground in the seaside town of Brighton. Within a couple of hours, they were no longer neutral and made love on the beach, oblivious of the shingle and, later, the waves as the tide turned.

It was a whirlwind romance that lasted two weeks, their studies forgotten. Neither had previously experienced such raw and wonderful feelings for another person. The chemistry was just right.

When they returned to Oxford, they managed to contain their passion sufficiently to proceed with their studies. But there was still adequate spare time to indulge their new-found love.

Loup tried contacting Deborah twice during his time in Switzerland. It seemed as if he was no longer nursing any hurt pride at being turned down. When Loup returned to the University to be awarded his degree, the three of them met briefly and were polite but that was all. Deborah and Daniel congratulated him and they had a desultory drink afterward. Loup caught the next plane to Switzerland.

The first signs of aching bones showed up in the spring of 1970, but Debs simply shrugged it off as having indulged in too much alcohol. When Daniel left in the summer of 1971, to complete his final year in Boston, Massachusetts, Deborah wanted to throw in her studies and join him, but he convinced her that she had come so far, it was important to continue. Even for his powerful intellect, the course proved very intense for

Daniel. Yet, they managed to find two weeks together to roam through the Eastern Seaboard of the United States; they both fell in love with Massachusetts. Daniel obtained a job with a prestigious American company even before he had graduated. There, he excelled and then was poached by a prestigious pharmaceutical firm in Lyon, France.

The following year, Deborah went to Lyon to complete her final studies. It was tantalizing to be so near to Daniel, yet she persisted with her academic work and she too was a success. Daniel attended her degree ceremony in Oxford in 1973. That evening, their celebrations were cut short as she buckled up with pain. But the pain went away and later they celebrated her job offer with the same firm Daniel worked for.

From time to time, Deborah suffered excruciating pain in her limbs, but the doctors could find nothing wrong. The pair excelled in their work, and they even heard that Loup was doing well too.

A freak accident at sea claimed the lives of both of Daniel's parents and he inherited a great deal of money and several business interests. He immediately set up his own pharmaceutical firm and, in the summer of 1979, Deborah and Daniel were married. Everything seemed wonderful but their honeymoon was spoiled by severe bouts of cramp in her legs.

It took several trips and a number of years to see an assortment of specialists before any firm diagnosis could be obtained. These were rough times, Cat's father had confided. He was often away on business, trying to keep everything afloat, and also seeking medical advice. "For a brief, so very brief time, we seemed to lose our way, my dear," he confessed. "But, finally, all was sorted out and Debs and I drew closer, after all."

Shortly afterward, they discovered that Deborah was suffering from a rare bone cancer, Schaffer-Neumann Syndrome. There was no cure, and the only consolation was that it was slow-acting. The following day, after this shocking diagnosis, they learned that she was expecting a baby. Against medical advice, she decided to take it to term and prayed the child would not inherit her problem.

Catherine was born on 12 August 1985, and was given dual citizenship, French and British. Two years later, her mother was confined to a wheelchair. Both Deborah and Daniel continued to work at their laboratories. They were successful in bringing five new drugs onto the market but the all-important cure for Deborah's ailment eluded them.

Then in 1990, they were contacted by Loup after a very long silence. By chance, he had recently heard about Deborah's condition and believed he had a viable cure, though the drug wasn't fully tested or cleared even for trials. All three agreed it was worth the risk. Loup's drug brought immediate relief to Deborah. But the respite was short-lived, as was she destined to be. Within eighteen months, she was dead at age thirty-nine.

"The autopsy determined that her chest bones had crumbled, and she had suffocated," Cat said. "I was seven as I stood at my mother's graveside."

"That must have been awful for you, Cathy," Rick consoled.

"Yes..." Her eyes felt surprisingly dry. If it wasn't for

her precious photographs, she feared she would forget what her mother looked like.

Over the years, building upon his parents' business, Loup Dante created a prestigious empire, Ananke, which he named after the Greek goddess of inevitable necessary force—Necessity and Compulsion—which seemed to echo his attitude. Many of his contemporaries considered him, virtually, a "force of nature" who permitted nothing to stand in his way. Over time, Ananke's expansion grew until it was responsible for creating and marketing cosmetics, perfumes, pharmaceuticals, plastics, biodegradable plastics, food supplements, and health foods. Ananke offices and laboratories could be found in Seahouses, Southampton, Geneva, Barcelona, Tangier, Shanghai, and Sicily, among other smaller concerns.

"Ironic, really," Cat went on, "but the cure for Schaffer-Neumann Syndrome was patented by Papa's Pharma in 2004."

"Tragic," Rick said. "Tragic."

"Yes..." At some point in the telling, they had lain alongside each other on top of her bed. "For comfort's sake," she'd said. She felt comfortable with Rick's presence; he was non-threatening, not demanding, simply listening attentively. Unspoken, yet implicit, his manner told her he would not take advantage of her. She snuggled up to his chest, hearing his gentle heartbeat, and willed herself only to tell him the bare bones. She owed him some explanation, after all.

"Well, two years later," she continued, "I went to Oxford to study chemistry." She'd traveled on her passport but, as a French citizen, she didn't require a student visa. "After graduating, I had intended taking up a position in Papa's firm. Unfortunately, about a year before my graduation, his firm was the subject of a hostile takeover by Ananke. Someone had betrayed him and he lost thousands of pounds as the value of the shares tumbled. He travelled around the country, trying to secure funds to block Ananke. Our family solicitor told me later that my father was about to sign a deal that would have saved him and the firm..." She faltered though she hadn't meant to but those days were still raw, still hurt. She heaved in a big breath and said, "But Papa died in a car crash in the south of France before he could sign. The other car involved left the scene and was never located."

She ended in a matter-of-fact tone: "That was in 2009; he was fifty-seven."

Rick held her hands in his but said nothing. She appreciated that; empathic silence helped.

"After the funeral, I learned that Papa had signed all the necessary papers for the takeover to go ahead in case he hadn't obtained sufficient funds to block it. Ananke took over, asset-stripped Papa's firms, sold some on, and closed others down, leaving huge debts and dozens of staff jobless. Once the outstanding debts had been paid, I had little money left."

Her eyes awash and vision blurred, Cat said, "Over my father's coffin, I vowed that one day I would get even with Loup Dante and his Ananke corporation. I was a realist and knew it might take a few years. But I would be patient." She forced a smile. "Like you, really."

"I can understand your reasons, Cathy. But..."

She placed her fingertips over his mouth. "Let me finish." Her lids felt heavy. She was tired. "Of course, I needed to finance my vendetta, so I left chemistry. I felt guilty at letting down my parents, but I worked hard, with long hours, and built up a lucrative career as a model." Through her dual citizenship, she obtained a British passport under the name Catherine Radley Gledhill, a professional name she'd established. "You see, modeling gave me the freedom to travel, to earn and to learn...certain things..."

Chapter 7

Worrying a Bone

S he woke with a stiff neck which wasn't surprising as she was lying on the bed alongside Rick, her head on his shoulder. Her heart fluttered for a brief second until she realized that she was fully clothed, as was he; he'd kept his promise. She blushed, remembering when she had undressed him. That seemed a long time ago. Considering she'd admitted to drugging him, he'd taken it all pretty well!

He was still fast asleep as she eased herself into a sitting position, adjusting the dress on her shoulders.

There were still so many questions buzzing around in her head. Why did he have a revolver in his safe and was it legal? Had he brought it here with him? She shuddered at visualizing, again, Zabala's holstered weapon. Was her obsession going to get her killed? Sure, she might be breaking—or bending, in her view— the law, but what she did should not warrant her death, should it?

She moved off the bed, leaving Rick to sleep. Déjà vu? Except there was no guilt this time.

As she slipped on her shoes, she paused and chuckled. Where the hell was she going? This was her room, her bed!

Gently, she held his arm and shook him awake.

He looked quite endearing, rubbing sleep from his eyes, fingering those long eyelashes. "What time is it?"

"Time you went to your own room—before some of the girls get the wrong idea!"

"I wouldn't want to tarnish your reputation, Cathy."

"I was joking. They'll all be dead to the world. It's always like this on the last night before the final shoot."

He sat up, swung his legs around, and put on his shoes. He stood, strode to the chair, lifted his jacket, and shrugged into it. "What happens after the shoot winds up?"

"We go our separate ways."

"Which, in your case, is?"

"Home."

"All this time, you've never told me," he said. "So, where's home?"

"You're persistent, aren't you?"

"I can be when it's important to me. Well, where's your home?"

"Alverstoke, Gosport..."

"Isn't that near Portsmouth?"

"Yes. Hampshire. Why?"

"I've got friends there, in Portsmouth."

"Small world."

"Are you going to invite me to your home in Alverstoke?"

"I'll think about it." She opened the bedside drawer,

pulled out her small bag, and withdrew a card. "My phone number. Guard it well."

He took it and saluted. "With my life."

"I hope not, it's only a phone number. It can always be changed if I get pestered by cold callers or stalkers."

"You can be so matter-of-fact sometimes, Cathy."

"It's my scientific training, you know."

He smiled ruefully. "I'm sure it is." He glanced at his watch. "Sleep tight for the next four hours..."

"Three—we're up early. Last shoot has to catch the dawn. And then they have to pack up the equipment..."

"You're a martyr."

"No, merely a model earning a crust."

"Oh, you're a lot more than that. I don't think Dante realizes how much danger he's in, you know."

"From me?"

"From your—or rather, our—crusade."

She rested her hand on his. "Then you meant it? You will help me bring down Dante and his company?"

"You have my word, Cathy."

On the impulse, she kissed him but didn't let it linger. "Thank you."

He raised a hand to his lips. "And you missed my nose... Maybe we're made for each other?"

"It was just a kiss to say 'thanks', Rick. Nothing more."

London

Zabala's rough kiss still burned on her lips as Petra reclined naked on the bed, smoking a Sobranie cigarette and still suffused with the afterglow of extreme passion. She watched him stride across the bedroom in his boxer shorts, trying and failing to contain his temper. "If that bastard hadn't interfered, I could have forced her to come with me!" he fumed. He reveled in violence, she knew. She wondered what kind of force he would have used on the woman. "Then I would have made her tell me everything..." He glanced over at her. "More information, I need more!" He slammed a fist into his palm and she flinched in expectation.

Earlier in the evening, he hadn't been too pleased when she showed him on her phone the video of the Outlet 5 break-in. "Why didn't Mr. Dante mention this?" he demanded. "I'm his head of security!"

She shrugged. "You were aware of the break-in. For some reason, he doesn't want pictures of the woman intruder broadcast, so he must have kept it from you."

He stopped pacing and swung around. "But it's her, the same woman who stole the documents! Emma Golightly!"

"Emma...?" She puffed out smoke and sniggered.

"What's so funny?"

"Where'd you hear that Golightly name?" she asked.

"She told me—at the plant office."

Petra chuckled and took another drag of her cigarette. "She was lying." She blew out smoke. "The little minx!"

"Lying?" he grated. And now, he stopped his pacing and let out a grunt of annoyance.

"Her name's Cathy Gledhill. She's a model. I met her—"

"You know her, the woman in that video, yet you do nothing?"

"Mr. Dante told me it was 'hands off' her for the time being…"

Petra mused that for her it certainly hadn't been 'hands off' for him. She'd enjoyed his rough sex.

"I need to know where Gledhill lives," he said, "what she plans to do next."

Petra blew smoke into the air. "Calm down, Emilio. She's a model, for God's sake, nothing more. For some reason, she's got a bee in her bonnet about our company. An animal activist, a pain, nothing to worry about. She's insignificant. Forget her!"

"Insignificant! She's caused trouble at least twice, already." He paused and snapped his fingers. "Perhaps she was responsible for the fire in our Angers plant, no? That was mysterious—"

"Arson was never proved." She shuddered. "It was a shock, I admit. Thank God, nobody was hurt!"

"It could have been her—or one of her accomplices who raided Outlet 5."

"Could be, of course… So what?"

"She is not insignificant, that's what! She uses a false name—Golightly! Yet Mr. Dante seems to be barring her from my inquiries. Why won't he let me deal with her?"

"Sometimes, I think he doesn't approve of your methods." She took another inhalation from her cigarette. "I do, of course. I like a man with a ruthless streak."

Arms akimbo, his muscular midriff pronounced, he smiled at her comment. Then, he shook his head. "No, there's something else, something he isn't telling me. It's as if he knows her. But that's not possible. I've been with the company for years and she's never shown on our radar."

"How would you know? Both her names—Golightly and Gledhill—are new to you."

"I've seen the employee photos..." He snapped his fingers. "Of course, I thought I'd seen *him* before!"

"Who?"

"Rick Barnes, the company lawyer! He's the man who rammed my car!"

She sniggered again. "I'm not surprised he's with her. He was her escort when I met him at—"

"Sometimes, you're so annoying, Petra. You hold things back from me!"

"Not knowingly, my dear. As it happens, I did a thorough search of the files at the time. Cathy Gledhill raised no flags at all. Even if she raises your temper." She chuckled fruitily. "You don't fancy her, do you?"

He snorted. "Don't be stupid! She's a brainless model. *Dios mio*! I prefer my women to be smart and attractive not simply pretty bimbos." He took a step toward her. "I prefer women like you."

"You say the loveliest things, Emilio." She stubbed out the cigarette in the bedside ashtray. "Come back to bed." She lay back across the unkempt bed and arched her body. "Show me how much you prefer women like me." And for added emphasis, she offered a come-hither pout. "Now, I promise not to hold back anything..."

Seahouses

Sitting upright at her desk, Mrs. Hannigan pouted her lips in disapproval while studying Detective Inspector Pointer over her bifocals. "Inspector, I can't understand why you would want to bring up that. The case was closed some two years ago. An unfortunate accident."

"There may be a connection with another case, Mrs. Hannigan," Detective Sergeant Basset explained.

"What case? I'm not aware—"

"I can't divulge that at this stage," Pointer said with a frozen smile. "You understand?"

"Very well. But it's all most mysterious."

"That's what we deal in, mysteries," Basset elucidated unhelpfully.

Pointer offered a sympathetic smile. "If I could, I would take you into my confidence, Mrs. Hannigan."

"Thank you for that, Inspector." She glared at Basset, shook her head, and pursed her lips.

"Can you provide me with all the documentation on the Ambrose accident?"

"Yes, of course. It will be in the storeroom." She pointed to the second door on their right. "I'll get it for you." She stood.

"Most kind," Basset said.

Mrs. Hannigan hesitated and then said, "That's if it's still where I left it!" She walked to the door, opened it, flicked on a light, and disappeared from view for about five minutes while the rustling of paper and slamming of drawers signified she was searching.

Eventually, she emerged, three thick folders in her arms, all smiles. "Thank goodness for that—it's all here though a bit dusty."

Basset pounced. "What did you mean earlier? Have files been going missing?"

Mrs. Hannigan blushed, eyes darting to the filing cabinet. "Well..."

"Please be frank, if you suspect files are going astray," Basset urged tenaciously as if worrying a bone.

Mrs. Hannigan dumped the folders on her desk. Motes of dust flew up from them. She wafted a hand ineffectually as she resumed her seat at her desk. "I had a visit from a private enquiry agent yesterday..."

"Go on, please," Basset insisted.

"She was with two members of the local action group—"

"Which group is that?"

"Defenders of the Sacred Earth; DOSE, they call themselves. They've been meddlesome in the past but seemed to have gone quiet recently, thank goodness."

Basset stared. "And...?"

"One of my files went missing. I noticed when they left." She produced an A4 notepad from the desk drawer. "This was put in its place. By the time I realized a switch had occurred, I was too late to stop them at the gate."

Basset relieved her of the notepad. "Did you contact the police regarding the theft? It hasn't been brought to our attention."

Mrs. Hannigan shook her head. "I wanted to but one of my superiors advised me not to bother." She shrugged. "He made a good case for not reporting it. After all, almost everything in the file is backed up on computer."

Basset nodded. "Very sensible."

Pointer added, "Were the contents of the file sensitive?"

"Yes, I believe they were—company sensitive."

"Which agency did the inquiry agent represent?"

"Bradbury & Hood."

Pointer eyed Basset. "Know them?"

"I do, actually. Shall we pay them a visit, sir?"

"Yes, I think we must." Pointer stood, extended his arm across the desk and they shook hands. "If I come across your missing file, I'll be sure to let you know."

Basset leaned put the A4 notepad on top of the pile of folders and then lifted them all from the desk.

Pointer scribbled a note in his pad, tore out the sheet, and handed it to Mrs. Hannigan. "This is a receipt for your dusty files. We'll return them as soon as we've completed our inquiries."

"Without the dust, of course," Basset added.

AT 10:00 AM, Rick walked out of the hotel carrying his suitcase. He wore the same suit as last night (Cat reflected that men could do that without any qualms). But now, he'd decided upon a light blue open-necked shirt. She'd opted for comfort for the journey and had chosen a mint-colored blazer with three-quarter sleeves and matching trousers with a yellow short-sleeved blouse. Yellow court shoes with two-inch heels gave her more control of the pedals than high heels. She pulled up in her car, her window open. "Give you a lift?"

"I was going to hire—"

"Where'd you like to go? Wales?"

He frowned. "Why Wales?"

"What you said last night, about Zabala. I can do sums, you know. I think that adds up to where you're going."

"I thought you had a final shoot."

"Done and dusted, probably before you woke up. Where in Wales, again?"

"Near Barmouth."

"Oh, yes. Off the A494," she said, grinning. "That's where I'm going. Are you coming?"

"All right. Is there space—?"

She pinged open the trunk.

He walked around to the rear. "I'll squeeze my cases in though you haven't left me much room."

"Be warned, I don't travel light. Anywhere."

He shut the trunk, dashed to the passenger door, opened it, got in, and sat. "Suitably warned." He slammed the door shut.

"There's no need to slam the door, you know?"

"Sorry."

"Maybe it's a man thing. Anyway, how's your car?"

"I rang Robson's, a local garage, and they sent a fellow around first thing to pick up the keys. They'll deliver it to my apartment when it's fixed."

"That's excellent service!"

"I thought so, too. A name to remember, I think." He clipped on the seatbelt and looked at her, gray-blue eyes playful. "Well, what are you waiting for? Aren't we going to Wales?"

"Here." She handed him her smartphone. "I've keyed in the destination—you can use the route planner app."

RICK NOTICED how confidently Cat drove down the A1, bordering on the speed limit, and easing back as he warned her about an upcoming speed camera indicated on the app. He was still trying to fill in the blanks about her past. Even after all the time he'd known her, she'd never opened up as much as last night. But he could tell by the way she reminisced that she was giving him a heavily edited version of her past with her father. A tragic past. In contrast, his childhood had been uncomplicated, simply wonderful. So they kept their talk to work-related subjects and that suited him fine. "It's quite boring being a company lawyer with few high points."

"Like an accountant, perhaps?" she offered.

"Good God, no, I'm not *that* boring am I?"

She giggled. "I don't find you boring at all. I mean, we've known each other for ages it seems to me."

That comment pleased him.

She drove through Newcastle upon Tyne, across the River Tyne road-bridge, through Gateshead. Shortly thereafter they passed the imposing and iconic Angel of the North, standing sixty-six feet high with a 177-foot wingspan, greater than that of a Boeing.

The road became the A1(M), a motorway.

By the time they reached the Wetherby Service Area at Junction 46, Rick's stomach was rumbling; Cathy must have heard it because she turned off and parked.

There were several outlets to choose from; they settled for pre-packed sandwiches—cheese and ham for him and Coronation chicken for her—and Costa coffee. While they ate and drank at a small table, Rick asked,

"When will Len break the story about the fake sampling reports?"

"I don't know. He keeps his contacts secret."

"I just wondered. Since the documents were obtained illegally, if Ananke gets wind of it, there'll be a court injunction to stop the publication."

"That's possible, of course. I suspect Len will have contingency plans. The idea is to hurt Ananke or even shut them down. They're powerful, though, so I suspect they'll use any legal loophole they can think of."

"Believe me, I know they will."

"The ball's in Len's court for now. Our site of interest has now switched to Ananke Wales."

"If it is Ananke."

They bought, for the journey, a couple of bottles of still water at the newsagent WH Smith and then didn't linger as they had about three hundred miles to cover.

Soon, they joined the M1 and then he alerted her roughly a mile later to merge onto the M62. She said she liked motorway driving though, around these parts, she had to keep her wits about her. He reckoned she had no problem with her wits—or anything else—but decided not to say so.

At junction 18, they joined the M60, and then back on the M62, and then the M6 and M56, with no holdups at all. Yes, you did need your wits about you.

As they approached the Chester Service Area, he said, "Not far now. Do you want me to relieve you for a spell?"

She straightened her arms and bunched her shoulders. "Yes, let's stretch our legs and get another coffee. Ten minute break."

"You're a harsh task mistress. Ten minutes it is, then!"

Wales

Cat was glad of the break. It was a hot sunny day and she removed her jacket then put it on the rear seat on top of Rick's.

When they left the service area, they continued along the A494 and soon passed Queensferry Bridge and the signpost to Conwy.

Throughout the journey, she had glanced at him from time to time and liked what she saw. She'd been on several dates with him though, at that time, she had viewed him as a man in the enemy camp. Now, she considered him in a different light: he was on her side. And, surprisingly, that felt good.

He broke into her thoughts, "This part of Wales is our family's old stomping ground."

"Yes, you mentioned that."

"Tal-y-bont camp caravan site," he mused. "Sand-dunes where we played hide-and-seek. A red starfish and a hermit crab in the rock pool. Even saw a lizard on the wall of a field, once!"

"Good, warm childhood memories. I had them... Though mostly I remember Papa—"

"Should I change the subject? I don't want to—"

"No, they're memories, Rick. Precious. It's good to bring them out and dust them down from time to time. Makes them fresh, bright, and clear again."

"Yes, I suppose it does, looking at it like that. My

parents and then my grandparents—when my parents weren't able to get away from work—brought Holly and me. We stayed at Barmouth, went for walks, and visited Harlech Castle. Yes, we did all that nature study stuff." He smiled at the memory but kept his eyes on the road. "Holly and I had great fun... Yes, I got to know the place pretty well."

They arrived at five in the afternoon. "There seem a lot more mobile home parks now," he declared.

"That's progress for you."

On the approach to Barmouth, he turned off onto an unsurfaced B-road and the car bumped along. "Hope this doesn't knacker your car's suspension!"

"I'm sure it'll be okay. Keep it in low gear."

"Yes, ma'am!"

She playfully punched his arm.

"Hey," he mock-yelped, "mind the pilot, we don't want to crash!"

After a while, she heard, across the fields, what sounded like generators. She opened the window; the sound was coming from somewhere ahead of them. "Can you hear that?"

"Yes. We're close. Just in time to pop in for cream tea and scones!"

Presently, the road became narrower, its gravel surface pitted with many potholes. On either side were occasional huge gorse bushes and a few animal tracks led off left and right. Telegraph poles stalked along the side of the track, the only sign of civilization.

They passed a couple of rough track entrances to unkempt fields then, finally, the rutted road led up to metal gates with electronic controls. The land was entirely fenced off. "I don't see any cameras," Cat said.

"You've got something about surveillance cameras, haven't you?"

"Lately I've become camera-shy. When you've been caught on one, you don't want to let it happen again."

Rick carefully reversed along the gravel road and swerved down a bumpy track, among gorse. "It should be out of sight here. Let's have a closer look." He got out and pocketed the keys.

Cat followed him, treading carefully in her court shoes. "At least it hasn't rained recently," she observed thankfully.

Within the boundary fence, there was a small-holding nearby. "That seems to be where the sound of the generators is coming from," she said.

Directly ahead, and to the right of the small building, was a gravel parking lot—four vehicles, including a pickup and, unmistakable with a dent in the rear, Zabala's blue Renault Fluence.

Further to the right was a long single-story shed constructed of corrugated iron; it seemed quite new, the paintwork around the window-frames unblemished by salty air or time. The sloping roof revealed three skylights on this side, maybe more on the other. A telephone line stretched from the roof at one corner across the parking lot to a telegraph pole. A wooden boardwalk ran all around the long shed, save for the far end, near the car lot; here, suddenly, the double doors rolled open and an unmarked truck drove out, its load covered by a grimy tarpaulin. It approached the gates which slid open on rollers and then, automatically closed after the vehicle had passed through.

"LET'S FOLLOW THE TRUCK," Rick said.

"Why?"

"Either its destination or the driver might tell us what Zabala is up to. I'll drive."

They rushed over the uneven ground to the car, and he drove northwards until, eventually, the truck pulled into a roadside café on the A494 a short distance outside Ruthin.

Rick parked close to the truck. "I want to save my phone battery," he said. "Have you got a torch I could use instead?"

"Yes. Glove compartment."

He removed it and they both got out. "Keep an eye on the driver, Cathy."

"All right." She sauntered toward the café's entrance door. Through the big window, she glimpsed the driver queuing at the counter with a tray. The server piled food on his plate, heaps of mash, baked beans, and sausages. He'd be busy with that lot for a while she reckoned and retraced her steps. Nobody else was about in the parking lot she noted, on approaching the truck.

Rick had already lifted a section of tarpaulin and crawled under it.

"Can you see anything?" she whispered.

"Oh, yes..."

Cat kept eyeing the café. Her nerves seemed to stretch. She checked the rest of the vehicles again but there was still nobody else around to take an interest in what they were doing.

She breathed a sigh of relief as, finally, Rick clambered out, clutching something to his chest. He stumbled as he landed then righted himself.

Her hand steadied him. "Are you all right?"

"Yes, I'm fine but let's get back to the car."

Once there, he unlocked the Hyundai and opened the trunk.

"Will you tell me now, Rick, and cut out all this suspense? What did you find?"

He held up three chunks of what appeared to be dried clay and stone. "The bed of the truck's crammed with big rubber buckets and they're all filled with nuggets of gold, just like these..."

She nodded, now recognizing the rocks. "So, they're mining illegally!"

"I believe so. And these are the proof." He flung them into the trunk in a small space next to his suitcase. "That truckload alone could finance Ananke for months—if Dante knows about it. Then again, maybe it's one of Zabala's little lucrative sideline activities?"

"Shouldn't you be aware of this going on, I mean, as the company's lawyer?"

He shut the trunk. "Not really. I only know what they tell me." He pursed his lips and then seemed to come to a decision. "I need to go back, have a look at the mine."

Her stomach squirmed at the idea. "Why?" she asked. "We could phone the police, get them to inspect this truck and its load."

"But I'd be willing to bet the driver's got fake papers to explain it."

"Or maybe it *is* legal?"

"No, I'm sure paperwork would bamboozle any copper called in at short notice. But the fact is that the Crown Estates own the rights to all precious metals in the UK and Ireland. They license all gold mining. And

I know, for a fact, that all of it in this area is licensed to Gold Mines of Wales. Think about it. If it was legal, there'd be signs up—instead, it's anonymous."

"Yes," she said, "that makes sense. You know, exposing this could seriously hurt Ananke. Let's get back."

When they returned, he parked in the same place. When they got out, it was clear that the temperature had cooled so they both put on their jackets.

"What now?" she asked as they stood, studying the layout.

Over on the eastern side, there was a gulley and water was being pumped into it. The discharge pipe led from an opening in the side of the long shed.

The metal mesh fence wasn't much of a deterrent— less likely to cause comment, perhaps. It was six feet high with nasty barbed wire strung along the top.

"I'll go over that fence, scout around," Rick said. "I can probably get some photographs with my phone."

"No electrification," she noted. She turned to the car, opened the rear door, and removed the rubber mats from the seat well. She gave them to him. "Here, use these."

"Good thinking." They negotiated the clumps of bracken and stones to the fence. As they draped the rubber mats over the barbed wire near an upright post, her shoulder strap slipped off and the handbag fell to the ground. "If I'd known we were doing this kind of thing, I'd have brought more suitable gear and a utility belt."

Rick laughed.

"Keys," she said. He threw them to her, and she

went to the car, put her shoulder-bag safe in the trunk, locked it, and returned and gave him the keys.

"Stay here," he told her and clambered up and then over with ease, firmly landing on the other side. He checked his watch. "If I don't get back in two hours, call the police."

"Two hours? Why so long?"

"It's a mine. The tunnel may go some distance."

She checked her wrist: it was 6:49. "The owners might call the police anyway. You are trespassing, after all."

"When did that stop you?" he replied with a grin.

Chapter 8

"Cat got your tongue?"

Cat's smile lit up her face. "Fair point."

Rick turned and crossed the rough ground, wild grass, tufts of brush and weed, and the odd rock skulking with intent to trip him up. He was glad it was daylight; if memory served, this time of year hereabouts it didn't get dark till nine thirty or so. Plenty of time to scout around, take some photos, and get out. He still had Cat's torch if he decided to venture into the mine tunnel.

The day's sun had been hot. Sweat soaked the shirt under his arms and his back and it felt uncomfortable. He'd need a shower after this.

He passed a stack of planks, probably spares from the boardwalk construction. He glanced over his shoulder at the fence. Cat had moved out of sight; perhaps she'd gone behind those gorse bushes.

There were narrow windows that ran the full length of the shed; maybe it was purpose-built, not originally intended for secretive work. He felt sure it was secret because he had no doubt that the mining was clandestine. The parked vehicles implied there were people here so he needed to be very quiet, he reasoned as he stepped onto the boardwalk. Thankfully, the planks didn't creak. He crept to a window. On tiptoes, he could just manage to peer through; its frame was too small to climb through.

Despite late afternoon sunlight streaming in the windows, the interior lights were on, and bulbs suspended from metal eaves that spanned the corrugated ceiling. More daylight beamed down from a series of three skylights in the roof.

To the left, in the far corner, there was a port-a-loo, next to a partitioned office with a couple of windows looking out onto the interior, the desk, noticeboard, and cabinets visible. A chasm about five yards wide ran most of the length of the shed; it came to a natural close at the far end, where there was a door. The ground there was the same as he'd traversed: rock interspersed with tufts of weed and brush; the chasm was a dark gash he couldn't see into.

Straddling the chasm was a metal trestle. Against a wall near the door were stacked acetylene gas cylinders and torch hoses. Fixed to a metal upright was an electric winch; a metal box with a couple of big red buttons on it was attached to one of the trestle's legs. To the right, a generator chugged away. It was connected to a panel with electric cables plugged in; he guessed it probably operated the winch as well as the lights. Cables snaked over the ground and dropped into the chasm. He could hear another generator, further away, possibly at the bottom of the chasm. That made sense: a pump to drain the water from the mine, he reckoned.

Two men wearing yellow hard hats stood at the

chasm's rim and leaned against the trestle supports; they were peering down. They wore green rubber boots, leather tool belts slung around their ample waists, jeans, and T-shirts. The metallic structure retained the day's heat.

The hoist rose and one of the men pressed a thumb on a button and the hoist jerked to a halt. Rick spotted a large rubber bucket on the hoist's pallet. The two men swung it off. The same man pressed a red button and the hoist lowered. How many were involved in this mining process?

The more there were, the harder it would be to keep it secret. He suspected that Zabala kept the number of workers to a minimum. Four or six, maybe. However many there were, it was far too many for him to confront.

He'd seen enough, Rick decided. *I'm a lawyer, not an adventurer.*

Maybe he could arrange a court order, or even a warrant and a police raid. It might take some time to organize. Then again, these people weren't going anywhere in a hurry.

He turned and his stomach lurched as he faced a man pointing a revolver at him.

"I think you'd better come inside, mister." Beneath the man's salt-and-pepper mustache, an unlit cigarette dangled from his pale lips. He wore a hard hat too, and similar clothes to the others.

"I was just—"

"*Just* do as I say, sir." His voice held a definite Welsh lilt. "You're on private property."

"I didn't see any sign."

"The fence should be a good hint." His eyes were

dark, glinting, uncompromising. "Now, come on, this way, *move!*"

"Do I raise my hands?"

"You can if you want to, but I don't care." He sounded irritable. Rick wondered if that was because he'd been deprived of a smoke. "Right, mister, start walking to me!"

Rick nodded and started walking, his hands held aloft, but after a few paces he lowered his arms, feeling foolish. It's not as if he had a concealed weapon on him. He recalled the revolver in his safe; quick-draw Barnes? No, probably not.

The boardwalk creaked underfoot even though he trod carefully, doubtlessly due to their combined weight. He passed the gunman and went on, a horrible itch materializing in the center of his back.

They reached the corner of the shed and the gunman shoved him to the left, toward the door.

"Open it, go in."

Rick grabbed the handle. His mouth was very dry. Yet his hands were damp with sweat and almost slipped on the handle. He swung open the door and stepped inside.

"Caddell, Davies!" the gunman barked at the two men by the chasm rim. "Make yourselves scarce. You can knock off early!"

"Aye, Mr. Jenkins, thanks very much!" The two men turned and made for the far end of the shed. "We'll shut the doors on our way out!"

That was the exit the truck had used earlier. Rick's stomach gyrated as they reached the doors, shut them, and locked them.

The place exuded a damp, musty smell, overlaid

with oil and grease. Rick detected a kind of metallic burning odor too; the kind that might come from the bank of plugs and switches or the generators.

At that moment, Zabala's face emerged from the lip of the chasm. He climbed to the top of a ladder that just poked out of the chasm. He stepped onto the firm ground. "Ah, the gallant Mr. Barnes." He glanced behind Rick. "All alone, I see. Well, no matter."

"I found him outside," the gunman explained, "peering in the window, Mr. Zab."

"Thank you, Jenkins. Thank the Lord for smokers' break-time!"

"What are you going to do, Zabala?" Rick demanded.

"What, no *señor*? How rude."

"I see no reason to be polite when I'm held at gunpoint."

Abruptly, the barrel of the revolver slammed into the side of Rick's head and he slumped sideways, disoriented. He managed to retain his footing and raised an arm in tardy defense but there was no further attack. His hand brushed against his temple, and it came away with blood. His head throbbed. His legs felt weak, and he wanted to be sick. He was unaccustomed to sudden violence; hell, he was unaccustomed to any form of physical violence!

"You be polite," said Jenkins, "or I'll teach you manners."

"Never mind," Zabala said irritably, "let's take him to the gold-face and show him what he wants to know."

"But, Mr. Zab—"

"Do it my way, please?"

"All right. You're the boss."

"Exactly."

Zabala gestured at the ladder he'd ascended pain-filled moments earlier. "Go on, Mr. Barnes. Jenkins will follow with his gun so don't try anything silly."

Rick glared. Silly didn't quite cover it; he'd been stupid to come. He feared that perhaps his two-hour deadline for Cat was going to be the death of him. Blood drained from his face as he slowly walked on shaky legs to the edge of the chasm and looked down. Beyond the shadows, there was light, a rough-hewn surface, pools of dark water, and some sort of narrow-gauge rail line that vanished in a dark tunnel in the earth. He bent down, grabbed the top of the ladder, and carefully swung around, placing his left foot on a rung.

"Go on!" snapped Jenkins. "We haven't got all day!"

Obediently, Rick descended. The rungs were caked in mud; his hands were soon wet and filthy. His shirt and jacket clung to his sweaty body.

He reached the bottom and stepped to one side, aware that Jenkins kept his handgun aimed at him.

The ground here was a mixture of stone and mud and it seemed slippery, even treacherous. It was much cooler here too, maybe due to the dampness. Puddles gleamed, globules of oil creating rainbow colors on their surface. Insulated electric cables snaked over the ground, along the tunnel, beside a thick discharge pipe, doubtlessly from the water pump. A thin cable was attached at regular intervals to the tunnel wall at head height and low-wattage light bulbs dangled, illuminating the place.

"Wait for Mr. Zab," Jenkins instructed.

"I'm no criminal lawyer but you do realize you face a stiff penalty for owning an illegal firearm?"

"Who said it was illegal?"

Rick shook his head. "Have you been to prison before? I hear it isn't great, no matter what the press infers."

"Yeah, I've done time." Jenkins thrust the barrel hard against Rick's breastbone. "I don't intend doing any more, all right?"

"Going straight would make sure of that."

Jenkins swore. "Shut it!" His face twisted, eyes narrowed. "What I don't need is a damned lawyer preaching!"

"You'd think—"

He didn't get to finish. The gunman slammed a fist into his stomach and Rick doubled up in agony. Wheezing, he tried to ignore the pain but with little success. His eyes watered and he felt bile coat his tongue. God, he didn't want to be sick. Not here, not now, not in front of this ignoramus.

Rick straightened up with an effort.

Zabala reached the bottom of the ladder. He carried a length of rope over his shoulder. He glanced at the pair of them. "What's been going on here?"

"Lawyer was getting a bit lippy. I gave him some lip back."

"You must control your aversion to lawyers, Jenkins. It will be the death of you."

The gunman snorted. "I don't think so!"

"Take him to the gold, then," he told Jenkins.

"Yeah, boss." The gunman shoved Rick, compelling him to move forward to the right. And though the first few steps were agonizing, the ache in his gut seemed to ease after a while.

They must have walked for about ten minutes through a natural broad tunnel of rock. The sound of a generator grew louder, and he heard a pump siphoning off the water.

Zabala strode alongside them. "You might be interested to know this, Barnes. One of Ananke's employees was on holiday in the area. He stumbled on this place." Zabala chuckled. "Quite literally. It was in one of those rare dry periods. The water table had receded—a freak, perhaps." He waved at the mud, the puddles. "Cornelius—that was his name—he'd been involved in mining some years ago, before he joined Ananke. In South Africa. That was diamonds. But he knew his geology, all right. Found a seam, a rich seam of gold."

"That's far enough!" Jenkins barked, interrupting.

Rick stopped.

Ahead were two men, stripped to the waist, hefting gold ore from the spoil they must have earlier dug out of the rock face. Sweat glistened on their torsos as they lowered the chunks into a rubber bucket, one of four on a small metal railway cart. Over on their right stood the generator and a pump; nearby was a stand of metal shelves with various hand tools on them.

The pair noticed the newcomers and paused in their work.

Rick saw that Jenkins kept the revolver out of view. Not that the observation would do me much good, he mused. Four of them, one of me.

"Everything all right, Mr. Zab?" the taller one asked.

"Yes." Zabala glanced at his wristwatch. "You're supposed to finish in an hour, is that not so?"

"That's right, sir." He wiped a dirty forearm over his brow.

"I'm showing this gent around." Zabala thumbed at Rick. "Why don't you finish early? You'll still be paid in full for today's efforts."

"That's very generous of you, sir."

As the pair lowered their tools and trudged past Zabala, Rick was tempted to call out to them but the hard nose of the revolver in his side suggested he refrained from that or any other impulsive action. Again, Jenkins was careful to conceal the weapon as the two men passed.

When the pair had gone, Zabala broke the silence: "Where was I? Oh, yes. Cornelius was aware of the implications. He wanted his share. So he approached me. We came to an arrangement. Ananke would take over his find and he would be compensated."

"I don't suppose *we* could come to an arrangement?" Rick said.

"Oh, I think we can—very similar, in fact." Zabala eyed Jenkins. "Cover him while I attend to the rope."

"Aye, sir."

"Right, Barnes," Zabala said. "Lie on the rail track."

"You must be joking!"

"No, I'm deadly serious."

"What's the point?" Rick queried. "I'm no Pauline, and there'll be no trains running along here any time soon."

Zabala shook his head. "I don't know what you are talking about. But I will only ask you once more—lie down or Jenkins will hit you so hard you'll fall down!"

"All right, all right." Rubbing the gash on his head, Rick lowered himself between the metal rails and lay full-length on the wooden sleepers. His elbow and backside felt wet. That did not discomfort him as much as his predicament. What was Zabala going to do?

While Jenkins covered Rick, Zabala pulled the rope off his shoulder and bound Rick's torso and arms to the metal rails, threading the length under a sleeper or two, and tethering his arms by his side. Then Zabala produced an extremely sharp knife and cut a length off of the rope and tied Rick's feet as well. The rope was tight, constricting.

Rick still wondered what Zabala was planning. It didn't make any sense. Maybe it was some kind of torture technique? "You're wasting your time, Zabala, I've got nothing to tell you."

Zabala hunkered next to Rick and put away the knife. "You have nothing I want to know. When I leave you here, I shall go to Hampshire and pay your model lady a visit. Continue where we left off when you interrupted me in the parking lot."

Rick's stomach heaved and his heart tumbled. He gritted his teeth. He wouldn't give Zabala the satisfaction of any retort. But he feared for Cathy now and cursed his own stupidity for coming here.

Chuckling, Zabala shook his head. "What is this, Mr. Barnes? No more quips? How do you say, has the cat got your tongue? Never mind. It is unfortunate that Mr. Dante will have to hire a new company lawyer..."

"What are you talking about?"

"I am talking about your demise. I shall break it to him gently when I see him in Barcelona."

Oh, God, he meant it, too! Why tie me up if he was

going to kill me? "Mr. Dante will be heartbroken, I'm sure," Rick rasped.

"Yes, I'm sure he will be." Zabala stood and turned to Jenkins. "Switch off the pump."

"Aye, sir."

Oh, bloody hell. His heart thudded against his rib cage as Rick finally realized his fate: they intended to drown him here.

Jenkins splashed through puddles over to the generator and flicked a switch. The background noise of the pump was suddenly conspicuous by its absence. Now, Rick heard the drip-drip of water, the faint settling sound of earth.

"Early tomorrow morning," Jenkins said, "we'll pump the water out and then remove him, give him a good send off to sea..."

Zabala's lips curved. "That will be fine. I expected nothing less. Thank you."

Craning his neck, Rick eyed Zabala. "It'll be obvious my death isn't an accident. My lungs will be full of freshwater."

"That's right."

"But the authorities will be suspicious."

"Probably." Zabala shrugged. "It will not matter. You are not the first to meet this end."

"Poor Cornelius," Rick grated.

"Yes. And poor you." Zabala turned away. "Soon, Mr. Barnes, the lights will go out and you will die in darkness," he said over his shoulder. "In a tomb of riches." He started laughing and the sound echoed, receding as he and Jenkins walked back toward the ladder.

CAT DUCKED further behind the bush as a car carrying two men drove past in a pickup. They hadn't seen her and didn't stop. She breathed a sigh of relief and checked her watch. Rick had been gone twenty minutes, yet it seemed an age. Still carrying the rubber mats, she paced amidst the bracken. She felt so helpless and realized she wasn't used to this role. Working with a partner might have its compensations, such as bouncing ideas off each other and sharing concerns and danger but it threw her because she felt she wasn't quite thinking through all the angles. When she worked alone, she was thorough and planned ahead. and believed she left nothing to chance. The operation in Anger had worked perfectly. The Ananke plant had suffered a serious delay in production, costing it thousands if not millions of Euros, and no lives were put at risk—because she'd prepared the sabotage properly. The same applied to her break-in at Rick's office; she'd planned that over a number of days.

Voices scattered her thoughts.

Abruptly, she stopped walking and hunkered down behind a bush as two more men left the shed and climbed into a parked car. How many were left inside? Apart from Rick and Zabala. There was one more car and Zabala's Renault still parked.

She scanned the area, her mouth dry.

Nobody else about.

She wouldn't wait. It was too exasperating. Using the rubber mats for protection against the barbs, she scaled the fence, finding it awkward in her court shoes. *All I need now is to catch a heel in mesh!* Her forearms shuddered as took her weight and balanced at the top; then she swung her legs over and dropped through the air. She landed lightly on the other side and freed the rubber mats and left them on the ground this side for later.

Again, she checked the entire area.

Still nobody about.

In a crouching run, she crossed the open space, feeling conspicuous.

As she reached the boardwalk and paused to catch her breath, the lights inside the shed went out. Then she heard men's voices. She hurried and hid behind the stack of planks. Through a gap in the pile, she had a view of the boardwalk, the shed door, and the car parking area.

Her heart skittered as she recognized Zabala. He was with another man who fiddled with keys and secured a padlock on the door.

Zabala fished out a bunch of keys from his jacket pocket. "I'm going to pay a visit on a model in Gosport..."

Cat felt the blood drain from her face, and she involuntarily shivered.

"Lucky you, sir."

Cat gritted her teeth. *You'll be out of luck, Zabala!*

Zabala grinned. "Quite so. She's going to get quite a surprise!"

"Your Barcelona flight is still tomorrow evening?"

"Oh, yes, it's scheduled for six forty-five. I can deal with the model and make it in plenty of time."

That's what you think, Zabala!

Zabala's next words slammed into her like a truck,

knocking the wind from her: "You're sure you can handle the body first thing in the morning?"

Body? Oh, my God. Rick! No, no! Tears brimmed her eyes; she brushed them away with a sleeve.

"Aye, sir, we'll catch the tide. It isn't as if we haven't done this before."

"No, of course... There'll be the usual bonus at the end of the month for you, Jenkins."

"Thanks, sir." Then the man he'd called Jenkins gazed across at the fence where she'd climbed over and paused. He stared, a hand stroking his chin.

Her already bruised heart tripped, almost stopped.

"Something the matter?" Zabala asked.

Jenkins shook his head. "Probably nothing, sir. You go on. I want to check the fence for peace of mind."

"Very good." Zabala pivoted, jiggled his keys, beeped his Fluence, and then strolled over to it. He got in and drove out.

With his departure, Cat sensed her tension ease ever so slightly. But not entirely. She held her breath.

Jenkins strolled to the fence where he picked up and then fingered the rubber car mats. Holding them in both hands, he stood, gazed about, then shrugged and flung them over the fence. He took out a pack of cigarettes and lit up. Slowly, he made his way to the parking lot and the last vehicle. He got in, switched on the motor, and drove toward the gate which opened automatically on his approach.

Cat sank back against the pile of planks and let out a huge sigh.

Her hands trembled and her stomach roiled. If they'd killed Rick, then her only course of action was to go to the police at once. But she couldn't scale over that barbed wire without some serious damage. Maybe she could drag one of these planks over to the fence and use it to cross the barbed wire? Yes, then run back to the car and drive like hell.

Blast! The car keys were in Rick's jacket pocket. And her cellphone was in her handbag locked in the trunk. Her earlier thoughts were spot on; she hadn't been thinking straight.

Chapter 9

Cat On a Tin Roof

Immersed not only in complete darkness but also rising water, Rick strained against the ropes that secured him to the metal rails.

Within minutes, his chest hurt, and his wrists were sore.

He couldn't budge.

And he could feel the water glopping against his body. It was difficult to be certain, but he thought it was already lapping against his thighs and wrists. He lowered his head and jerked it up again; the water had touched his earlobes. He had to strain to keep his head up now. A crick in the neck was going to be the least of his worries.

He heard small splashing sounds and faint squealing. Something nudged his left thigh a couple of times. Christ, he was sure it was a rat! He shuddered as the thing's tiny feet scampered up his leg and over his chest. Then there was a splash near his head. And then the splashing ceased. He was alone again.

He had no way of knowing how quickly the water

139

seeped in. But he feared the rest of his life was measured in minutes rather than hours.

CAT FROZE, indecisive.

Think! Why hadn't Rick come out?

Because he was dead?

She wouldn't allow that thought to loiter and drain her resolve. Perhaps he was only hurt or wounded...or, God, dying. They'd left him to die? Would they be so callous? She recalled Zabala's gun in its shoulder holster. If someone carried a deadly weapon, then they must be capable of using it. But she hadn't heard a shot. Would she have heard it from outside the fence? Perhaps he used a silencer.

Think! How to get inside? She ran to the door. The padlock was big and unlikely to budge without immense force being applied. She cast about, scanning the area. No discarded tools and no stones of sufficient size and weight that she could use to smash the padlock from its hasp.

She glanced up. The black squares of the windows beckoned. But they were too narrow for her to squeeze through, even if she broke one with a stone.

Then she recollected seeing the roof and its three skylights.

She hurried around the building, seeking a way to scale up to the roof. She was an accomplished climber, after all. But its walls were prefabricated, sheer metal. Even barefoot, she couldn't hope to gain purchase on the rivet heads.

Her stomach flipped emptily. Time was pressing. If

Rick lay dying... *No, don't go there!*

RICK CONCENTRATED all his effort on his right hand. Clenching his fingers into a fist, he tried to raise it. There was the slightest give in the rope. Maybe the water had affected it? He relaxed and breathed out, though it was awkward, keeping his chin against his chest in order to keep his head out of the water.

He strained again and his wrist pained him as he raised the fist.

Perhaps it had moved a fraction more this time? No way of finding out. Relax, lower the hand.

Yes, he felt sure the rope had stretched a little; he was sure there was more give in it now.

He tried again. And again.

His wrist felt sore. When he lowered it into the water, the cooling effect helped ease the soreness and gave him the strength to try again. And again.

Rick gritted his teeth against the now constant pain in his wrist.

Must persevere. Must try again!

THINK! Cat was drawn to the planks she'd hidden behind. Simple! She ran over to the pile.

Hefting the top one, she realized it was too heavy to carry. Edging it off the stack, she let it fall and jumped out of the way as it clattered on the ground. Wrapping her fingers around the end, she lifted it and dragged it over the ground toward the shed.

She had to stop a couple of times, squatting, the end of the plank resting on her thighs. Her fingers and wrists protested, which surprised her since they were strong and used to tackling cliffs and the sides of buildings. Different tension, different pressure.

At last, she heaved he plank up on the boardwalk and rested it against the shed wall, below a window. Gradually, she eased it higher up the wall and then with all her strength lifted it a few inches and let it fall against the window. The pane shattered and shards were strewn everywhere on the wood boards.

Now, the plank rested on the windowsill.

Hurrying to the other end, she bent over and shoved it until she was confident that it wouldn't slip off the sill.

Carrying her shoes, she stepped onto the base of the plank. The wood was rough under her bare feet. Steadily, she walked up the slope, one foot in front of the other, arms extended on either side for balance.

The plank bowed under her weight.

Come on, I'm a model; I'm not that heavy!

She prayed it wouldn't snap. She kept going, stopping a moment when the plank seemed to bounce too much with her movement and then, as it settled, she continued, holding her breath for no good reason.

As she approached the top of the plank that pierced the window, she was eye-level with the edge of the corrugated roof.

Reaching up, she got hold of the corrugated surface and hauled herself up onto the ridged metal, glad to feel its firmness and stability.

Standing confidently, now more in her element, she walked up the roof's incline toward the nearest skylight.

As she went, she noticed the landscape was darkening. Night wasn't far off. The coast was visible from this vantage point; the breakers showed starkly against the dark sea, phosphorescent. The sea where Jenkins intended to consign Rick's body...

Don't dwell on that!

She reached the skylight and knelt beside it. At least this was big enough for her to clamber through.

Slamming the heel of her shoe against the window-pane, the glass shattered. She used the heel to clear any shards jutting out from the frame.

Then she lay on her stomach and peered inside.

Her heart sank when she realized how shadowy the place was. The last vestiges of daylight barely percolated through the various windows and the roof accesses. She had to get inside before it became so dark she wouldn't be able to see a hand in front of her. Brilliant planning, Cat: the damned torch was in Rick's pocket!

***

RICK THOUGHT his efforts were working, though whether it would be enough to prevent him from drowning was another matter. Slowly, surely, Rick stretched the rope around his right wrist until he felt sure he could pull his hand free. It hurt like hell as he squeezed his hand, fingers outstretched, rigid, thumb touching little finger, making the shape of his hand as narrow as possible. He tugged and tugged.

Abruptly, his hand was free.

Thank God.

But he couldn't see the ropes or detect any knots to

unfasten. And the rope strapped around his chest held him down, too.

He managed to shift on the bed of sleepers, the water splashing, and partly leaned on his side, so raising his head a little higher. He might have given himself a few more precious minutes.

Now what? Try the same method with the left hand?

His right was so sore there was no strength in it. If he had no strength in his hands, he couldn't hope to unfasten the rope securing his chest.

But he wouldn't give in, he wouldn't admit defeat.

Blindly in the pitch black, he forced his weak right hand to scrabble under the water, seeking any stone that might be used to sever the rope around his chest.

His fingers closed on what felt like a suitable chunk.

He lifted it out of the water and felt the stone's surface; carefully rotating it in his hand until he was satisfied with which part would serve as a primitive cutting tool.

One side was jagged, as if chipped, either by geological forces or a miner's implement.

Water lapped at his chin and the restraining rope on his chest prevented him from raising his head any further.

Using the stone, he began sawing at the rope on his chest, each cutting motion an agony, pain lancing through his wrist and forearm. His movement disturbed the water around him, and it splashed his face. He sputtered, spat out the gritty muddy muck, heaved in air, and coughed which made his chest ache even more.

His body wanted him to stop and take a rest, but he persisted for his life depended on it.

CAT SHOVED her shoes in her jacket pockets and, careful not to cut her hands on the bits of glass wedged in the frame, she lowered herself through the skylight. Her jacket snagged and tore; a shoe dropped and clattered below.

Suspended by her hands, she dangled there. Looking down the length of her body, she saw, about two feet away from her swaying toes, a metal cross-girder.

She let go and dropped, landing firmly on the soles of her feet, unbalanced then righted herself. All she had to do was walk the length of the girder to the wall.

Her soles felt dust and small granules of soil or stone that covered the girder, a potential hazard. She was aware of the night closing in, stopped and glanced around. Against the wall stood the electric panel—and beside it, the generator. She wasn't sure but she thought she heard water lapping. She wanted to call out to Rick but reasoned she'd better get down and put on the lights first. Up here, she couldn't help him—if he was still in need of help; *dismiss that idea!*—until she could see what she was doing.

With each step more confident than the last, her pace quickened and, finally, she reached the wall. From here, she easily clambered down the upright, its huge nuts and bolts offering purchase for bare feet and hands. At last, she jumped to the hard-packed earth. She found the fallen shoe, brushed the soles of her feet with a hand, and then put on both shoes.

Darkness increased suddenly. Must be a cloud scudding over.

She ran past the oxyacetylene trolley and stopped in front of the console. She flicked a couple of switches and the generator whirred into action and, seconds later, the overhead lights flickered on. And the chasm lit up from below too.

She scanned the interior. A small forklift truck was parked on the other side of the cleft in the earth. Several barrels of oil stood against that wall. But there was no sign of Rick and nowhere he could be hiding or lying. The office structure was a possibility, she guessed.

Then she saw the ladder that jutted out of the chasm. Beckoning.

She stepped toward it and leaned forward, hand on one knee. Dread gnawed at her insides. If she got no response, then she'd check out the office.

"Rick!" she called. "Rick, are you there?" There was a faint echo.

"Cathy!"

He was alive! Tears pricked her eyes. "Rick!" she croaked. Then, summoning a more firm, louder voice, she added, "I'm in the shed, by the ladder! *Where are you?*"

"Thank God! I'm at the end of the mine tunnel—come down the ladder. At its base, turn right! Hurry, *I'm about to drown!* Please hurry!"

JENKINS SAT in a booth of the countryside inn, holding his second tumbler of Penderyn single-malt whiskey. Under his breath, he swore.

I should have taken that damned lawyer's billfold! What was I thinking of? Bet he carries oodles of money.

Seems the type to flash it about. I bet there's no such thing as a broke lawyer. I could go back now. There was ample time. I could break him, yes, that would be nice!

He took another sip. The smooth liquid stilled his urgency.

No, it'll keep till the morning when I move the body.

He pictured again Barnes' face. Arrogant bastard!

Now, that Cornelius bloke, it had been survival, business as usual.

But that lawyer, he's got under my skin. *It's almost personal.*

He smirked, remembering his punch to the lawyer's gut. I enjoyed that! Should have hit the boyo harder.

I should hurt him some more before he drowns.

He checked his watch. Hell, it was only a half-hour drive.

Jenkins swallowed the rest of his whiskey and got up, headed for the door.

Outside, he felt the liquor sing in his veins. In anticipation.

He went to his car, opened the door, and sank into the seat behind the wheel.

The solid weight of the revolver pressed against his ribs. He looked forward to hurting the lawyer before the man drowned.

And, of course, the bastard was bound to carry plastic. Maybe I can force him to tell me his credit card PIN before he dies.

He switched on the engine, released the handbrake, revved up, and left the parking lot at speed.

Arrogant swine. He deserved all he was going to get!

Seahouses

Avril Bradbury opened her office door. Light from a streetlamp percolated through a window onto the landing. A man and a woman stood on the threshold. They introduced themselves, Pointer and Basset, explaining they were from NCA, flashing ID at her so fast she decided she must enroll in a speed-reading course.

"Thank you for seeing us so late," Basset said.

She eyed the clock: 9:38. Nighthawks. "No problem. I work odd hours, too." She closed the door behind them, moved to her desk, and sat. "Please take a pew." She pointed to the two chairs facing her.

They sat, Basset nursing a brown leather briefcase. Neither of them offered any pleasantry or smile. *Cathy Gledhill, what have you got me into?*

"Nice to see you, I'm sure. How may Bradbury & Hood help you? We've never had a visit from NCA."

Basset began: "Did you visit Mrs. Hannigan at the Ananke plant with two clients?"

So that's the way it was going to be, eh? Avril's lips pursed briefly, and she shifted in her chair. "Yes." It would be foolish to lie to these two.

Basset tapped her fingers on the lock of her briefcase. "For what purpose?"

"Didn't Mrs. Hannigan explain?"

"We ask the questions, Miss Bradbury," Pointer said forcefully.

"Of course you do, and you're doing a good job of it, I must say." She ignored the inflamed glares. "Well, they told me they were representatives of

DOSE and wanted to see the actual sampling of the waste product, to verify the monthly report readings. Mrs. Hannigan was in agreement, so I don't see—"

"A file went missing from her office." Pointer leaned forward. "After you and your clients left, she noticed it had been taken."

"Really? How distressing for her. But you said it was 'missing'. Is there any proof that it was actually *taken*? I must emphasize that, at all times, I was in Mrs. Hannigan's presence. I couldn't have taken it if that's what you're implying."

"She suspects your client, Miss Gledhill, took it."

"Oh, that's outrageous!"

"Miss Gledhill said she was pregnant," Bassett stated. "Is she?"

"I'm not a doctor, so I couldn't say. I believe she did suffer a bout of 'morning sickness' while we were there, however."

Basset said, "That's what Mrs. Hannigan told us too."

"I'm glad we have that corroborated, then." Avril glared at Basset and smiled without humor.

Basset opened her briefcase and held up an A4 notepad encased in a polythene bag. "This was left in place of the missing file. It probably has fingerprints on it."

"Do you have Miss Gledhill's prints, then, to compare?"

"Perhaps she's on record already," suggested Pointer.

"Perhaps, as you say. I wish you luck." She eyed the pair brazenly. "Anything else?"

Pointer stood and narrowed his eyes. "Have a care, Miss Bradbury. If you or your people—"

"My brother is the only other person in the firm."

Clearly exasperated over the interruption, he went on, "Don't overstep the line, Miss Bradbury, or the full weight of the law will descend upon you!"

She stood now, arms akimbo. "I'm suitably warned, Inspector. I trust you're as firm and forthright with real criminals. Knowing that is so will help me sleep at nights."

"Good evening." Pointer pivoted on his heel and stormed to the door.

Basset followed, almost barking at his heels.

The door slammed shut.

Avril opened the bottom drawer of her filing cabinet and took out a tumbler and a bottle of Black Rory whisky. She poured a good measure and sipped it, then returned to her desk.

She sank into her chair and thought, *I've just been savaged by two bloody dogs!*

Wales

Cat's yellow court shoes were caked in mud from the edge of the chasm, and she slipped awkwardly a couple of times on the rungs as she descended the ladder but held on tight. When she reached the bottom, her feet plunged into swirling brown water that reached just above her ankles.

Steadying herself on the ladder, she turned right and splashed through the cold muddy water.

Within minutes, it was up to her calves.

She stumbled many times and also stubbed her toe: the obstructions felt hard and straight, maybe metal rails under the surface.

Then she heard high-pitched squealing and dark brown and pale gray shapes jumped out of the gushing water onto rocks at the side of the tunnel. Rats! But wild, not like those she'd seen in her father's laboratories. There were four or five; she couldn't count them as they moved too swiftly. They ignored her and simply headed toward the other end of the tunnel.

"I'm coming!" she yelled.

"Hurry, Cathy!"

There was a gradual curve in the tunnel and then, suddenly, her throat felt dry, not with exertion but shock. Rick was lying on his back, almost entirely covered with the murky water; only his right arm, his head and part of his chest were above the surface. She spotted a band of partially severed rope over his chest.

He sputtered. "Hurry, untie the ropes!"

As she moved toward him, she slowed, scanning the tunnel.

"The knots are under water. I'd never find them or might not be able to unfasten them now that they were wet. There isn't time, Rick!"

Then she saw the generator. "The pump!" she exclaimed and waded toward it, flicked switches and the pump began chugging away. It probably wouldn't lower the water level, but it might buy them time by preventing the level from rising.

A metal shelf on the right held tools of all sorts, all dirt-clogged. These people didn't care for their equipment. She splashed over to it and gave a start as she spotted a rat in a corner hiding between a hammer and a screwdriver. Seeing her, the rat jumped off the shelf into the water with a splash and swam away. She hefted a weighty chisel. She was careful not to lose her footing as she approached him; she didn't want to stumble now and pierce herself or Rick, even if the damned chisel appeared quite blunt! "I'll try to cut the rope!"

She knelt by his side, pressed the dulled edge against the rope that was already frayed, and began sawing at it. "This is the sharpest tool I could find!" she explained.

"It's cutting, keep at it!" There was desperation in his eyes.

Abruptly, the rope snapped apart. He heaved his body and forced his chest above the water. "Thanks, Cathy!" He gasped and sputtered. "My other wrist's still tied... And ankles..."

"We'll have you free in a jiffy," she promised and stepped over him to tackle the left side.

———————

JENKINS FROWNED. His car's headlights lit up the cut-off from the road. From here, he could see the long shed.

The lights shined through the windows.

But he'd definitely switched them off.

He turned onto the rough track and the car jounced over the potholes.

Somehow, the fuckin' lawyer must've got free!

Slowing the vehicle as he approached the entrance, he fished out the control from the glove compartment and pressed the button to open the gate.

Chapter 10

"Let slip the dogs..."

Seahouses

Sergeant Basset knocked on DI Pointer's hotel room door. He answered almost at once. His face was grim. The interview with Avril Bradbury hadn't gone well and he'd been desultory over their evening meal. They'd decided the stolen file was none of their business. Nothing in the Ambrose files suggested foul play, either.

"I know that look, Sergeant. What have you found out?"

"Sir, my search has flagged another suspicious death relating to Ananke. Drowning. The body found at sea off Bardsey Island, Cardigan Bay. Name of Brynn Cornelius, age forty-two."

"What's his connection to Ananke?"

"He was a manager in their jewelry division."

"Jewelry?"

"Ananke diversified some years ago." She playfully

tweaked the gold studs in her lobes. "Jewels and perfume go together, didn't you know, sir?"

That forlorn look appeared in his eyes again and Basset regretted her comment. "Sorry, I didn't mean to—"

"It's all right, Sergeant. Plenty of water has washed under the bridge..." He stopped and smiled ruefully, as well he might, she mused. Water had been his problem.

"You said the death was suspicious."

"Yes. He was drowned in fresh water—well, muddy water, actually."

"But didn't you say he was drowned at sea?"

"No, he was found at sea, having drowned."

"When was this?"

"Last September."

"And the coroner's verdict was 'unlawful killing', I presume."

"By person or persons unknown. And still unknown, sir."

"And his family was never in the frame, I suppose?"

"No, sir, he was single, a well-traveled man who hadn't really settled anywhere for long."

"I see. You're going to suggest we travel to Wales?"

"I've booked a hotel at Barmouth, sir. That's where the very late Mr. Cornelius was staying."

"Very well." He sighed. "But it sounds like a wild goose chase, probably totally unconnected to our investigation."

She grinned. They were a good team. She'd heard the odd whisper: "Let slip the dogs of law!" was a phrase attached to them.

His eyes lit up. "I know your hunches of old,

Sergeant. They're valuable and not to be ignored. I'll get packed."

———

Wales

Soaked to his skin, Rick clambered up the ladder. His sodden jacket seemed to weigh him down but that wasn't only the muddy water; he'd pocketed a couple of gold ore chunks.

Cathy followed him.

As they reached the lip of the chasm and stood under the ceiling lights of the long shed, he let out a chuckle.

"What's so funny?"

"We both look a sight!" He waved a hand at his soaked and bedraggled suit. "It's ruined."

She grinned. "And they say women are vain about their clothes?"

"You're a sight for sore eyes, Cathy, truly." He took a step and embraced her. It felt good to hold her. Not so many minutes ago, he feared he was going to die. "You saved me."

She gently pushed him away. "We're not out yet." She glanced up at the shattered skylight. "I don't think you could scale up to there."

He shook his head and massaged his sore wrist. "No, not even if I felt one hundred percent—which I don't."

"Stay here. I'll see if I can find something we can use to force the door."

Cat left him and picked up a spade that rested against the wall by the door. She hefted it and smiled at him.

He felt all in but managed a token smile back. Then he remembered. He pointed at the corner office. "The phone—we could call the police."

"And how'd we explain being trespassers breaking in?"

"But—"

Suddenly, she held up a hand and signed for him to be quiet.

What the hell?

THE GATES SLID OPEN, and Jenkins drove through, pulling up in the gravel parking lot. He got out and ran to the double doors that faced the entrance; they were still padlocked.

Taking out the revolver, he ran to the boardwalk and mounted it. Fuckin' hell. What's going on here? A plank leaned against the shed wall and was inserted in a broken window. He pounded the boards around to the far end of the long shed. The single door was also padlocked.

Maybe he'd been mistaken. It had still been daylight when he left, after all. But who'd moved that plank? Nobody could have climbed through the small window.

He pocketed the gun and dug out his bunch of keys.

Time to beat up a lawyer.

AT FIRST, Cat thought she'd been mistaken but, no, it was definitely a car engine; tires crunched on gravel. Somebody was coming back.

Seconds later, there were footsteps pounding on the boardwalk outside.

She heard the rattle of keys and the padlock being released.

Her heart racing, she signed to Rick to be quiet.

A man opened the door and stepped inside.

"Jenkins!" Rick yelled, presumably to distract the man.

"You'll not stop us now!" Cat screamed in frustration while swinging the spade at the man's head.

Jenkins ducked to one side and the blade slammed into his right shoulder. He swore and backed away then he pulled out his revolver, wincing at the effort. "Steady, now, honey, or—"

A couple of chunks of gold ore hit him in the face, thrown by Rick. Jenkins staggered, dropping the gun before he could shoot.

Jenkins backed away further, dodging another swing of the spade, and stumbled against the trolley that held the oxyacetylene gear. He wiped the blood from his face with his left hand and glared. Then he hastily grabbed the acetylene torch. "Right, you're both going to burn!"

Awkwardly, he fumbled in his pocket and took out his lighter. His lips curling in dark amusement, he ignited the blowpipe.

Immediately, the flame sprayed toward Cat from the blowpipe but the torch also made an odd squealing sound and, in the same instant, the flame also flashed back up his arm. Jenkins' grin transformed into a high-pitched screaming rictus. He dropped the oxyacetylene torch and staggered against the cylinders.

"Rick," Cat called, "use your jacket—douse the flames!"

In seconds, Rick rushed Jenkins and covered the man's flaming arm with his wet jacket.

Jenkins shrieked.

"Out, let's get out!" Cat shouted, pushing Rick and Jenkins ahead of her toward the open doorway.

Cat and Rick supported Jenkins between them as they tottered outside. "Get well clear—the parking lot!" she urged.

Trembling with shock, Jenkins mumbled something in Welsh and lost consciousness. The sudden dead weight unbalanced the pair and they all fell to the ground.

"Stay down!" Cat snapped.

Abruptly, a massive explosion erupted inside the shed, lifting a portion of the roof near the doorway. A gas cylinder sailed into the night sky some fifty feet, a contrail of flaming gases in its wake; then it plunged somewhere in the cleft of earth where the mine's water had been pumped.

The shed continued to burn, black noisome smoke rising against the starlit sky. No more cylinders mimicked missiles.

Cat sat up and brushed stray hair from her face. "That was close," she croaked. The smell of singed material and burnt flesh hit her nostrils, all coming from Jenkins.

Clearly in pain, Rick got to his knees. "Well, we're out..."

"Yes, just." She glanced at Jenkins, searched his pockets, and pulled out a cellphone. "Mine's in the car and I guess yours is ruined?"

"Yes... We can't stay here. I may have great faith in the legal system, but we can't escape from the fact that we're trespassing..."

"True." Kneeling beside Jenkins, she eased his unconscious form into the prone position and then unsteadily got to her feet. She helped Rick to stand. "Besides," she added, absently brushing down her clothes, "we need to follow Zabala to Barcelona."

"Barcelona?" He shook his head. "You can't seriously think about going after Zabala now. We were both almost killed tonight!"

"There's no 'we', Rick." She rested a hand on his shoulder. "It's *my* obsession. I'm sorry it nearly got you killed."

"No, you saved me—twice. How'd you know about the explosion?"

"Acetylene is unstable. A flashback like that could have exploded in Jenkins' face and even killed him. These people seem to treat their tools badly. That torch should have had a flashback arrestor fitted; maybe it did, but it didn't function. As for the cylinders, usually they won't result in an explosion, if the fire department can get to them in time and douse them with water for a few hours, it'll be okay."

"Usually?"

"Sometimes, the cylinder can explode in a matter of minutes and even launch itself through a brick wall."

Rick shuddered. "Christ."

She pressed a key on the cellphone, and it lit up. "I'll call for the fire brigade and an ambulance." She didn't know the precise location, but the pall of smoke would be obvious to the emergency services from the main road. "Then we'll go."

Between them, they carried a plank to the fence and rested it on the top then scaled up and over.

She got the keys off Rick and opened the Hyundai's trunk then unzipped her suitcase. Swiftly, she stripped off her jacket, blouse, and trousers. The night air was cool and gave her goosebumps in her bra and briefs. She put on a lightweight sweater and jeans, dumped the ruined clothes in a corner of the trunk, and put on a pair of trainers. Beside her, Rick changed also, putting on a fresh shirt and jeans though he fumbled with the buttons because of his sore wrist.

She passed the torch over them; it revealed that their faces were dirty—smoke- and mud-smeared. Dried blood clung to Rick's temple.

"We need to get away now," she said. "We'll clean up at a motorway service area."

It was 10:45pm when they left the site. The black smoke was still spiraling into the night sky. Cat drove as Rick's wrist was too sore to be safe. By the time they were on the main road, the sirens were strident, getting closer. Minutes later, the fire engine and an ambulance raced past, going the other way. "Jenkins doesn't deserve saving," Cat said.

"Knowing what he's done and planned to do, I tend to agree with you, Cathy. But my lawyer brain tells me to let him undergo a trial."

"You're probably right." She then concentrated on the road, taking her lead from his instructions, heading toward Welshpool, then Oswestry and Shrewsbury. They stopped at the Telford Welcome Break Service Area on the M54. Here, they cleaned their faces and hands in the restrooms, then grabbed a snack of sandwiches, cake, and coffee. By now, it was gone eleven and they agreed to find rooms at the Days Inn.

Arranging for an early call at seven, they retired to their rooms. Tired and aching, Cat simply wanted to tumble into bed but she was glad she didn't. The shower was invigorating and she felt much better after it.

Unpacking her nightdress, she donned it, sank into bed, and immediately went to sleep.

Next morning, over breakfast, she confided, "Zabala said he was going to my home."

Rick swore. "He must have got your address from the hotel records."

"Probably. But, whether he's there or not, I have to go there, to get my passport."

"I don't think he'll hang around. Once he finds you're not at home, he'll move on."

"Let's hope so."

They set off at just after 8:30 am.

Hampshire

Three hours later, their stomachs rumbling, Cat drove on the approach road to Lee-on-the-Solent, remembering in time to slow down for the speed camera on the bend. Then, the expanse of the Solent water was there on their right with the Isle of Wight and the white sails of yachts. Normality. The Jenkins and Zabala nightmare was already a dim memory. She opened the window and let in fresh ozone-filled air. Home, almost.

They stopped at the Inn by the Sea and enjoyed a simple meal of chicken Kiev followed by caramel apple Betty and custard for dessert.

Suitably fortified, they set off for the final stretch, passing what used to be the Ministry of Defense's Browndown firing range, now turned silent. She turned onto the Stokes Bay coast road and thence into her street in Alverstoke.

"I can't see anybody loitering," she said, peering through the windshield. She pulled into the drive of her two-bedroom townhouse, in front of the green garage door.

She turned off the engine.

Gingerly, they got out, neither shutting their door. "Leave the cases," he whispered.

Rick went ahead of her, approaching the front door warily. It was locked. He waved her over. She inserted her key and pushed open the door. The alarm didn't beep. "I'm sure I set it," she whispered. "I always do."

Rick pushed past her, flicked on the hall lights, and quickly strode along the hall to the kitchen.

She checked the alarm box; it wasn't set.

"The back door's been forced!" he called.

The impact of those words hit her with the potency of a taekwondo foot in her gut. "Oh, no!" The sensation brought back memories of a misjudged practice kick and that time when the family had been burgled shortly after her mother died. All the security that she took for granted was abruptly torn away from her, whipped out from under her feet. She felt awkward, unsure of her balance.

When she got to the kitchen on her shaky legs, she had to lean against the door frame.

The kitchen cupboards had been searched, the tins, condiments and boxes strewn on the countertops. Some had spilled to the tiled floor, burst open and messy.

"Was it a burglar, do you think?" she croaked. "You read of the dreadful things some of them do to people's homes."

"No, I reckon this was Zabala. He must have disabled your alarm system."

"How—what's the point of an alarm if the crooks can do that?"

"Most burglars are amateurs, even opportunists. So my father says, anyway. Clearly, this Zabala is an expert."

She nodded. "At Seahouses, he said he was Head of Security..."

"That explains it, then. Few can protect themselves against a determined professional."

"I think I'm going to be sick."

Avoiding the detritus, she rushed across to the sink unit, leaned over it, and turned on the cold tap. Bile rose to her mouth, flavored with garlic, and her stomach heaved; it was as if she really had sustained a blow there. One hand holding her tummy, the other she cupped under the stream from the tap and washed her face with the cool water. Thankfully, the wave of nausea passed. She didn't really want to throw up in front of Rick.

"Are you all right?"

She straightened and nodded. "I suppose we'd better see what he's done to the rest of my home." She prayed that Zabala hadn't found her hideouts. But, if he was a professional, as Rick implied, he might well have done so. She rubbed a hand over her face, which was still wet. *Steel yourself.*

Tenderly, Rick wiped her face and hand with a kitchen towel. Then, they walked from room to room, her hand in his.

The dining room served as her office; her desk drawers had been pulled out and the contents thrown on the floor, paper, bills, photo-shoot proofs, and letters. The computer monitor and tower were untouched, it seemed.

In the lounge, the display cabinet's drawers had been tipped out as well. The television and DVD player were still there.

"You're right, this definitely wasn't a burglary," she said.

"I wonder what he was looking for?"

She shrugged. "I can't imagine."

They climbed the stairs. Her cheeks burned with rage as she picked up discarded panties and bras from the treads.

When she got to the landing, she shoved the underwear in the laundry basket and entered her bedroom, fearing the worst.

Her floor-to-ceiling closet doors swung wide open; her expensive clothing was in disarray and many items had been thrown on the bed or the floor. Then, her heart did a flip as she noticed some photo album pages protruding from under the bed. With a fearful heart, she knelt and pulled the album out. Her vision blurred as her fingers brushed over the pages—a good number had been torn out and, even after a frantic search, were nowhere to be found. Distraught, she wondered what Zabala wanted with photographs from her childhood, pictures of her, her mother, and her father. It felt like some kind of desecration, even worse than the distasteful handling of the contents of her lingerie drawer.

Fuming with barely suppressed anger, she grabbed the underside of her bed and tipped it up.

"Cathy, what...?"

She managed a faint grin. "He didn't find the safe." She pointed to a square cut into the floorboards here.

Kneeling beside it, she inserted a finger in a knot-hole and pulled up the square of board to reveal the countersunk safe. She spun the dial several times and then opened it and took out her passport, spare money, and jewelry.

She regained her feet and felt her body tremble.

Rick was there, crushing her to him. "It's awful, I know, but it will pass. We were burgled about ten years ago. Dad was furious, of course. He felt sure it was one of those felons he put away. Mum and I didn't want to live there anymore but it was impractical to move. Besides, we felt—"

"I know." She dipped her head into his chest. "We were robbed shortly after Maman died... Papa felt the same then. He said, 'Why let some lowlife scum force you to move?'"

She pulled herself free. "One more thing, first." She went over to the left-hand open closet and fiddled with a catch on the side wall. A wall door clicked open.

"Come into my parlor," she said, stepping inside.

She flicked on the light to disclose a familiar small room. Directly in front of them was an entire wall filled with cuttings and photographs of Loup Dante. On the right-hand wall was a peg-board pinned with pictures of various Ananke establishments, all of them indelibly committed to her memory.

"My God," Rick said behind her, "you *are* obsessed with him, aren't you?"

"Yes, I am." She gestured at the Loup Dante wall. "I got a lot of the pictures from the Internet—the society sites. Others, more recent, from *Hello, OK, Hola* and similar celebrity magazines."

He walked past her, studying the pictures, pointing. "Looking at these, it seems he's had three brides. There's no mention of them in the brochures or PR stuff. That's strange; I work for him and yet the impression he gives is he's a single playboy."

"None of the marriages lasted very long," she said. "Apparently, he arrived at an amicable financial settlement with each divorce."

Rick stroked his chin. "I wonder what 'amicable' means to him?"

"I shudder to think."

Glancing around, he whistled, thumbing at the third wall on their left. "You seem to have quite a collection here." Hanging there was her climbing equipment, a powerful bow and a quiver of arrows, a selection of martial arts weapons and, leaning in the corner, her parachute pack and a large kite.

Nothing she needed right now. "I need to re-pack for hot Spain, Rick."

"And I need my passport."

Richmond upon Thames, London

It was a two-hour drive to Rick's apartment in Richmond, which was quite familiar to her. She flushed warmly, thinking it seemed an age since she'd drugged him and stole his security combination number.

As a matter of priority, Rick made a few landline phone calls. One was to a contact, Sol Stein.

Within the hour, Sol arrived at the apartment. Rick made cursory introductions.

Sol was in his fifties, compact, with a hawk nose, bright eyes, and no hair. He blinked repeatedly as he spoke.

Rick handed over the three chunks of gold ore they'd brought in from her car's trunk.

Sol whistled. "This is good quality, my lad." Blink, blink. "Welsh, I'd say." Blink, blink. "Where'd you get it?"

"A slight acquaintance. He was going into the mining business but decided it was too risky. Got his fingers burnt, actually."

Cat barely hid a smile at that.

"These were his samples," Rick ended.

Cat marveled at Rick's glib response.

When Sol left, Rick explained, "Sol will give me a fair deal. I thought maybe we could use the money in our vendetta against Ananke."

She kissed him lightly on the cheek. "*Our* vendetta. I like the sound of that."

He touched his cheek. "And I like the feel of that."

"When this Spanish jaunt is over, maybe...?"

"Maybe more?"

She nodded.

"I can work with that. I'm happy to keep my distance, as it were, frustrating though it can be."

"Most honorable of you."

"I get a charge just being with you, actually." He grinned, and then added, "Speaking of charge..." He dug out an old cellphone from his desk. "It needs charging but it'll do till I can get a new one."

He used the landline to telephone Gatwick and was pleased to get two seats for the 18:50 flight. "It's going to be a rush."

Then, he rooted in another desk drawer and pulled out his passport and a little green book, which she recognized. "I wondered about that before," she said. "Shouldn't it be black?"

"I think it's meant to be eco-friendly. I inherited it from my father when he retired last year."

"Really?"

"Useful connections, shall we say. He was a criminal lawyer and managed to build up quite a collection of worthwhile contacts. 'I don't envisage you using it,' he said but he reckoned I might if I ever got tired of corporate law. He didn't think much of me going into the commercial side of things. I pointed out that it was where the money was and he simply said he preferred to put bad people away rather than feather the nests of rich directors."

"I like your father already."

"So you disapprove of my choice of profession too?"

"Not entirely. But I definitely side with your father about banging up crooks. They seem to get a better deal than their victims, every time."

He chuckled. "You sound like my friend, Leon."

"Leon?"

"Leon Cazador. He's a private investigator in Spain."

"One of your contacts in your little green book?"

"No, we met a while ago when I was on holiday. He helped a friend who inadvertently got caught up in something shady..."

"Leon sounds intriguing. I bet he's on my wavelength."

"I don't take bets." He grinned. "He detests the ungodly, if that's what you mean."

"The ungodly, eh? Sounds like he won't be too fond of Ananke. Will I get to meet him?"

"Most certainly. He's quite a character. On the way, I'll fill you in on his CV, well, what he's told me. I've asked him to arrange a hire car for us at Barcelona airport."

Spain

Barcelona nightlife enlivened him, Zabala thought. He sat opposite Dante in a discreet corner of a nightclub, complete with subdued lighting and scantily-clad waitresses and waiters—all tastes accommodated.

He licked his lips, but he wasn't thirsty. He proffered a large brown envelope. "You will be interested in the contents, I think."

Dante opened the envelope and slid out a few sheets and pages that had been torn from a photograph album. His eyes widened. "You haven't hurt the Gledhill woman, have you?"

"No. She wasn't at home when I called. The paperwork I obtained is of interest, also."

Stuffing everything back in the envelope, Dante said, "I'll read it all later." He sipped his Torres brandy.

"How is the project going?"

"Profesora Quesada reports that the tests are progressing well." Dante smiled. "I'll pay her a visit tomorrow. What do you plan to do? I see you're not drinking."

Zabala glanced around, eyeing an attractive darkhaired dusky-skinned waitress. "No, I want all my faculties honed for this evening. I think I will amuse myself greatly."

"You know, Emilio, from time to time, you have the uncomfortable habit of making me wish I had never asked you a particular question."

"Really, sir?"

"Yes, and this is one of them. Don't enlighten me further on your plans for tonight. I'll see you at the facility tomorrow."

"Yes, sir. I will be there."

Wales

The night staff busied themselves with quiet efficiency at Dolgellau and Barmouth hospital. Detective Inspector Davies was stout, cheerful, and obliging. He showed Pointer and Basset into the patient's room. "Mr. Jenkins says a lawyer started the blaze."

"Really?" Pointer said.

"That is so, sir, it is," Jenkins croaked. His right arm was completely bandaged, and that side of his face was red, almost raw. He'd lost some hair and the remainder was singed. He winced as he spoke. "His name was Barnes. He was from London, I think."

"Interesting," said Pointer, nodding. "Not very law abiding of him, was it?"

Sergeant Basset added, "And you work for Ananke, is that right?"

Jenkins hesitated and then glanced at his billfold on the top of the bedside cabinet. "I do, yes, I do."

"What business is—or rather, was—Ananke conducting?" Basset persisted, a dog gnawing at a bone.

"M-m-m—that's a trade secret." Jenkins jerked his head at DI Davies. "I want a lawyer before I say any more."

"But," chipped in Basset, "not Mr. Barnes, I presume?"

He glared at her. "Sod Ananke. You should be chasing Barnes. He's dangerous!"

"Thank you, Mr. Jenkins," Pointer said. "We will find Mr. Barnes, be assured." He turned to DI Davies. "Book Mr. Jenkins on a charge of illegal mining, for now."

"Hey, you can't—!" Jenkins snapped, leaning forward, his lips slavering.

"Oh, yes, we can," Basset assured him.

"And," Pointer added to the DI, "see if you can get hold of the others involved."

"Already on it," Davies replied with a smile.

"Good work. And you might want to obtain a

search warrant for Mr. Jenkins' house. You may find something relating to the mine."

DI Davies smiled and nodded.

"Hey," Jenkins snapped again, "you can't—!"

Basset leaned close to him and whispered harshly, "But he can, Mr. Jenkins. And he will."

Chapter 11

Catalyst

London

Rick's secretary, Mandy, checked the caller through her door's security peephole. There were two people standing on her porch: a man and a woman. They seemed impatient.

A short distance away was a uniformed policeman —a rare sight these days. For a moment, her gut somersaulted. She hoped her parents were all right.

No, a death wouldn't bring three people to her doorstep, surely? She glanced at her watch. It was late. The man held up a warrant card to the spyhole. This must be important.

Removing the chain, Mandy unlocked the door and opened it a crack. Clasping the collar of her white toweling bathrobe, she peered out. "Can I help you?"

"I'm DI Pointer and this is DS Basset from the National Crime Agency. We're sorry to bother you at this late hour but the security man at Ananke head office referred us to you."

Mandy nervously patted her curly platinum-blonde hair. "You'd better come in." She stepped to one side to admit them into the hall. "I've just had a bath."

"Again, our apologies," Pointer said.

She glanced around the door.

The policeman hovered outside.

"Doesn't he want to come in?"

"He's happy to wait there," Basset said.

"All right." Mandy shut the door and padded ahead of them in her fluffy slippers and led them into the lounge.

She indicated a sofa and sank onto an armchair, tucking her legs under her. She turned her cornflower blue eyes on them. "Crime Agency, eh? What's all this about?"

"We're trying to locate Mr. Barnes," Basset said.

"What's he done?"

"We cannot divulge that," Basset said. "We need to eliminate him from our enquiries."

Mandy smirked at the phrasing that was so glib and meaningless. "The last I knew, he was up in Northumberland..."

Pointer nodded. "He was. But no longer."

"Then I can't help you."

"Where does he live?" Basset persisted.

"Ah, I see. Our night security man was being very cautious. I see that now. He wouldn't disclose Rick's address. As his secretary, it's up to me..."

"That seems to be the case," Basset said. "Most diligent of the man." She didn't sound too pleased concerning the security guy's thoroughness.

"Well, I can oblige. Certainly. Rick's apartment is in Richmond on Thames." She swung her legs down, got

174

up, and sashayed to the bureau. "I'll write it down for you."

"There's no need," Basset said. "I have a good memory."

I bet you have!

Mandy told her.

Spain

Loup Dante arrived at the Ananke facility in the center of Barcelona with Petra Grimalkin and was immediately met in the foyer by his Spanish male secretary who informed him in hushed tones about the fire at the Welsh gold mine.

Dante ground his teeth together. "Leave us!" he snapped at the secretary and stepped into the elevator, Petra close on his heels. He stabbed the penthouse button with a finger, glaring into space. He didn't utter a word; the atmosphere in the cubicle was tense.

Alighting from the elevator, Dante stormed into his office and slammed his briefcase on his desk. He swung around and eyed Petra. "This is like Angers all over again! It must be that woman!"

Petra frowned. "You can't be sure, sir?"

His eyes lanced. "I don't believe in coincidences. Too many things have gone wrong. First, Angers, then Southampton, now Wales..." He glanced away, noticing his hands were trembling. "My God, if she is... No, she can't be!"

"Sir?" She was concerned now; he was beginning to

ramble as if obsessed with the Gledhill woman. But why?

"I need to know, to make sure..."

"What do you need to know, sir? Please tell me and I will do all I can to—"

"I have to... You can..."

"Sir? What do you want me to do?"

He sank back in his chair, a hand covering his eyes. He shook his head in a resigned manner. "Get Zabala, bring him to me."

A thrill ran through her at the mention of Emilio's name. She suddenly didn't want to be in the Gledhill woman's shoes, designer labeled or not. "At once, sir."

London Gatwick

Early evening in Gatwick was subdued. There seemed less hustle and bustle. Cat knew it was an illusion, yet people seemed to run down like clocks as dusk hovered, even if the concourse was brightly lit. Both were familiar with the heat of Spanish June and had dressed appropriately for comfort and style. She wore an Emilio de la Morena black outfit, trousers, low-cut top and bolero-style jacket, with black shoes. Rick had opted for a blue short-sleeved shirt and matching stone chinos.

They sat at a small table, sipping coffee. From here, she could watch the overhead monitor.

"Cat, what do you know about Ananke's Barcelona operation?"

"Not a lot. You mentioned your nose was useful for the perfume division."

He sputtered over his coffee and chuckled. "Yes, I remember...only too well. That's harmless, a good money-maker, I'm sure..."

"Oh," she added, "and Dante is there for the final clinical tests of the Catananche product. Some drug or other."

Rick whistled. "So, you know about Catananche, I see!"

"Your safe's paperwork was helpful, up to a point," she replied sheepishly.

"Ah, of course. Those documents didn't cover the final clinical testing, though."

"The documents didn't tell me very much. Actually, I overheard Dante discussing it with his pet, Petra, over cocktails."

"She admires him, but she isn't his pet. I think she prefers younger men. Men with power."

"I didn't like her. And I don't think you do either."

"Not a lot passes you by, does it?"

"I try to keep my wits about me."

"So I noticed."

"I've just noticed, too, our flight's boarding." Cat pointed to the monitor indicating the 18:50 British Airways flight.

As she got up, she remembered those times when flying with her father to a holiday destination, times when she'd been full of anticipation. Now, it was a different kind of anticipation, something that clutched at her vitals and promised to be fraught with danger.

Richmond upon Thames, London

The local constabulary gained access to Rick's apartment by using a spare key supplied by the building's superintendent. The entrance was backed up with a warrant, obtained due to Mr. Barnes' link to the Barmouth mine fire.

Pointer and Basset searched while the constable stayed in the corridor on watch.

They found smoke-and mud-covered clothing on the bathroom floor. "Maybe Jenkins isn't spinning a yarn," Basset said.

"Maybe. But the trail has gone cold."

"They've gone somewhere," she observed. "His shaving tackle is missing."

"Perhaps he doesn't shave."

"Jenkins' description tells us that Barnes shaves, sir." She opened a desk drawer and added, "The contents have been riffled recently—some recent letters are at the bottom..." She pulled out a small photograph album. "These are a few years old, according to his scribble on the reverse but we may be able to use one of them for ID purposes?"

"Let's see how old the passport photo is. That might be more recent."

"I'll get onto it first thing in the morning, sir." She checked her wristwatch and looked at him meaningfully.

Pointer rubbed his chin. "All right, let's call it a night. You go home and pack a bag in readiness while I send out a check on all the ports and airports."

Barcelona, Spain

Cat and Rick's two-hour flight arrived at Barcelona El-Prat airport, and they adjusted their watches an hour ahead of UK. Now, it was 22:00. Passport control was no hassle, as expected.

At the baggage claim room, the carousels were idle while the cases were unloaded from the plane. A young woman was fussing with a trolley and berating, in English, her three-year-old who wouldn't stand still. Behind her, on the carousel, she'd left her infant lying on the rubber surface.

Cat accosted the woman: "Excuse me, but I think you should take your baby off this conveyor belt."

"Who the hell do you think you are? She's my kid, not yours!" The woman swore and turned on her son. "Behave, you little tyke, will you? Everybody's looking at us!"

At that moment, the conveyor motor started up and the belt moved.

The woman seemed oblivious as she tugged at her son's arm.

The emergency stop button was further away than the baby. "Oh, what the hell!" Cat said and quickly chased around the carousel and picked up the child. The baby smelled like her nappy wanting changing.

"Hey, what're you doing with my baby?"

"Saving her life, madam," Rick said. "Haven't you read about a mother whose baby died by doing exactly what you've done?"

Suitably chastised, the woman said, "Well, that's all right then." She brusquely took her daughter from Cat and stormed to the other side of the carousel.

Cat and Rick's luggage arrived early, and they loaded the two cases on a trolley and were quickly processed through customs.

At the arrivals barrier, Rick waved. "There's Leon."

Private investigator Leon Cazador was tall and broad-shouldered with dark brown eyes and a smart, short haircut that left a dusting of gray over his ears.

Cat recalled that Rick said Leon was born in 1963, so he was about twenty-two years older than her, yet he seemed younger than fifty-one, perhaps in his early forties. As he walked toward them, his tread appeared light, poised, and almost catlike. He shook hands with Rick, then her. His grip was firm but gentle, his smile genuine. He wore a lightweight tailored tan suit, no tie, and stylish brown loafers. "Pleased to meet you, Cathy."

Leon handed them a cellphone each. "Spanish number, registered. Use these rather than your English phones."

"Thanks, mate," Rick said.

Leon stooped to pick up her suitcase with ease. His hands were big and powerful. Unselfconsciously, he exuded sureness and strength. Cat imagined that he kept himself very fit. Probably, he maintained a regimen learned in the Spanish Foreign Legion and later their secret service; according to Rick, anyway.

"I have a car waiting—it isn't hired. Borrowed." He winked at Rick. "Not traceable."

"Thoughtful, but what makes you think we need to be concerned?"

"I asked a friend to flag any traffic about Ananke, as we discussed. It seems NCA is taking an interest."

"NCA? How do you know that?"

"DI Alan Pointer is an old friend, so we keep in touch from time to time. He was hospitalized a short while ago but he's back with the NCA now. He tells me they've put out an all points alert for you. Something about a fire in Wales."

Cat reddened. "Oh."

Leon rested a hand on Rick's shoulder. "Don't worry. Alan isn't aware that I know you."

"I don't want to make things awkward for you, Leon. Perhaps we should make our own way from now on?"

Leon shook his head. "I know you, Rick. And, more importantly, I trust you. We're both on the same side though perhaps not singing from the same hymn-sheet. My conscience is clear. From what you've already told me about Ananke, it seems to thrive on bending or even breaking the law. In my book, they deserve whatever they get."

Cat winked at Rick. "I told you."

"What was that?" Leon asked.

"Oh, just a private bet."

London

Basset leaned back in her office chair, a hand over the mouthpiece of her telephone. The glow from her computer screen highlighted her strained features. "Barnes flew out to Barcelona with BA at 18:50, sir."

"Barcelona, eh?"

"And he was accompanied by a woman, Catherine Gledhill."

"Interesting. Jenkins mentioned a woman was with him. It appears that those two are now acting as a team —first at Ananke Plastics and now in sunny Spain!"

"Thanks for the information," Basset said into the phone and then hung up.

Pointer rummaged in his drawer. "Which flight can we make?"

Basset's fingers flew over the computer keyboard. "I think we can get there in time for the 20:30 departure, sir." She clicked the mouse. "I've just booked it. Easy-jet." The nearby printer churned out their boarding passes and tickets.

"Very good, Sergeant. I'll get onto our Barcelona contacts."

"I hope they don't mind it being late evening pick-up."

"That's what they're there for, isn't it?"

She grinned and switched off her computer. "You'll need to take your sunscreen lotion for tomorrow, sir."

"I know." He took a couple of tubes out of the drawer and flung them on the desktop. "Don't remind me!"

Barcelona, Spain

Leon drove, the car's headlights cutting a swathe on the surface of the C31, which eventually took them via the bow-string bridge across the river Llobregat. He drove along the Ronda Litoral until he eventually turned off into Carrer de la Marina—Marina Avenue. The traffic congestion was dense, not eased in the least by the presence of a blue and white tram system that ran in its own lane and intersected the various roads. Leon was a very competent driver., even so, Cat was glad when he finally turned off the main street and entered a parking lot beneath a block of apartments.

He pulled up in a parking bay near the access doors to the stairs and elevators and switched off the engine.

Nobody else was about. A half-dozen cars were dotted about in marked bays.

Leon handed Rick the car keys. "I thought it best that you didn't stay at a hotel since you'd have to show your passports on registering."

Rick nodded. "I've always thought that odd. We don't do it in England."

"Perhaps you should," Leon said with a smile.

Rick stepped out and shut the door. "Presume it makes us traceable?"

"Yes," Leon said, getting out. "It's a legal requirement. Doesn't just apply to Spain, either. UK hotels seem a bit sloppy in that regard, perhaps. Something to do with its porous borders, I shouldn't wonder."

Cat exited, clutching her handbag, and glanced around. "Where are we staying?"

"There are a number of empty apartments in this block." Leon opened the trunk, took out their cases, and locked the car. "The modern story of Spain, I'm afraid, ever since the *crisis*—the collapse of 2008 all of six years ago. Spain has about three million unsold buildings. Many repossessed by the banks, who are hanging onto them to inflate their assets columns." He clenched his jaw, surely a sign of annoyance, Cat thought. "It's frustrating to many; they won't sell them off at reduced prices."

"And presumably there are plenty of homeless?" Cat said.

"Yes, of course. Too many people without homes and too many homes without people." He smiled thinly. "At least a few councils have warned the banks that they'll be fined up to 100,000 Euros if repossessed homes remain empty for over two years. A few others have even threatened that the banks will be compelled to hand over the properties for use as social housing."

"Good for them!" Cat cheered.

Rick shook his head. "Before the financial crisis, I thought lawyers were near the top of the *persona non grata* list. I suspect that spot's now occupied by bankers."

"I certainly don't trust them much now," Cat said.

"You may be right," Leon said. "As long as they get bonuses when they're blatantly seen to fail, then the public's attitude won't change. But it isn't only the banks that are responsible. A good number of empty properties were bought by mafia groups and crime cartels from Russia, China, and Romania. Other places have served to help launder money."

The elevator arrived and they rode it to the fourth floor. They walked along a carpeted corridor until Leon stopped at number 48 and lowered the cases. He fished out a key, unlocked the door, and ushered them in.

The place was fully furnished. He dropped the keys on the hall table, under a large gilt-framed mirror, while Rick brought in the cases. Cat shut the door and glanced around.

The apartment was immense.

"This place is empty?" she said. "It appears occupied."

"An estate agent friend acquired it last week," Leon explained. "It's available for rent, fully furnished, but he's had no takers. It's not surprising as the rent's too high."

"Who are the owners?" Rick asked.

"A Scottish couple who hit hard times; they wanted to retire here but the crash put paid to their plans. They both need to work longer, so their dream retirement is on hold. In the meantime, they want income from this place to make ends meet."

"I'll rent it," Rick said.

Leon cocked his head. "You don't know the cost yet."

"I have funds." He winked at Cat. "Enough, anyway."

"All right. I'll make arrangements so the paperwork can't be traced to you."

"It sounds as if you've done this kind of thing before?" Cat observed.

"I have a few bolt holes here—and elsewhere. Sometimes, I make enemies who bear a fatal grudge so it's useful to merge into the shadows."

"Oh." Looking at him, she felt sure he could handle himself but perhaps making oneself scarce was a healthy option. Maybe she and Rick would have to do the same before long. "How many bedrooms are there?"

Leon gestured at the doors leading from the lounge. "Three. I won't be staying, though. I have my own place, not far from here."

Cat looked at Rick and he returned her gaze openly. She felt sure his mouth curved just a little. She lifted her case and pointed to the door on her right. "*I'll* take this room."

"I'll have the one next to yours, then," Rick said, picking up his suitcase.

They both made for their rooms and came out almost at the same time.

"I'll unpack in a minute," Cat said. "I want to look around this place first."

"Me too," Rick said.

Leon gestured at the curtained French windows. "I might sound like a dreaded estate agent, but I can assure you that you've got a good view of the Sagrada Familia from the balcony."

"Really? How wonderful!" She drew the curtains and opened the door. Stepping out onto the balcony, she gasped. Diagonally opposite rose Gaudí's distinctive gnarled structure, the emblem of Barcelona, floodlit.

The city spread before them was a mass of colors, all vying for her attention. Traffic was heavy and loud, horns tooting, motor scooters screeching.

Leon and Rick joined her, resting their forearms on the metal rail.

"Each time I see it," she said, "I always find it both amazing and sad."

"Sad?" Rick queried.

"Gaudí lost everything in his desire to finish it. When he died, he was penniless, virtually a beggar."

"I didn't know that," Rick said.

"Cathy's right. The building relied on private funding and, toward the end of his life, Gaudí couldn't get financial backing, so he sold his family house at Riudoms to pay for the work. He stopped going to the theater and cafés and adopted the diet of a penitent.

Once a man of sturdy stature, he shriveled up so his clothes hardly fit him."

"Poor man," she said. "He must have been obsessed by it."

"Obsession can be a dangerous affliction, Cathy," Rick observed in a meaningful tone.

She shot him a puzzled glance. What did he mean by that? He was as obsessional about getting even with Dante, surely?

Leon went on, "When Miguel Primo de Rivera became dictator of Spain in 1923, he did everything he could to destroy Catalanism, banning the Catalan language, its dance and flag. Three years later, Gaudí died under the Line-30 tram and the onlookers mistook him for a tramp."

"But that was ages ago," said Rick. "Yet it still isn't finished."

"There were problems," Leon explained. "In the civil war, Anarchists burned Barcelona's churches and attacked the crypt of the Sagrada Familia, the site workshops. They burned his plaster models and every scrap of paper—plans, drawings, letters, everything relating to the building. Nobody to this day knows exactly how Gaudí intended to finish it. Yet, they're trying. It's hoped it will be completed on the centenary of Gaudí's death. For now, though, it's a glorious unfinished dream, though some critics regard it as a nightmare."

"Well, I for one like it," she said. "May he rest in peace."

Leon shrugged. "The mob opened the tombs and dragged out the skeletons and dumped them outside including, by some accounts, Gaudí's corpse, which was dragged through the street by a rope around its neck."

"That's so medieval," Cat said, shuddering at the image in her mind. "A bit like Richard III was mistreated in death."

"I think, even today, there's only a thin veneer of civilized behavior covering most of us," Leon stated.

"I agree," said Rick. "There were real fears that people wanted to disinter that awful child abuser Savile and scatter his bones."

"Well," Leon said, "I think they recovered Gaudí's corpse and reinterred it."

"Better than being buried in a parking lot, I suppose?" Rick said.

Leon's face turned somber. "I've seen worse treatment of the dead in war. And those sights don't leave you, either. They tend to harden you toward the ungodly."

Cat turned away. "Let's change the subject, shall we?" Then she smiled at them both. "I'm famished. Is there a restaurant nearby you can recommend at this hour?"

POINTER AND BASSET's plane landed at 23:35 Spanish time and, once they were cleared through the airport, it was midnight. At the arrivals barrier, a tall, slim blond man held up a plaque with their names scrawled on it. He introduced himself as Jonathan Bryson, an embassy representative. He was perhaps in his early thirties.

They shook hands and Bryson relieved Basset of her suitcase. "I've got a van parked outside. They're pretty reasonable about waiting time here but I don't want to dawdle."

"No diplomatic disc?" Basset teased, quickening her pace to match his long stride.

He grimaced. "Not this vehicle. I didn't think you'd want your arrival advertised too blatantly."

"Fair enough," Pointer said.

They passed through the doors and Bryson gestured at a white van, clicking the key fob.

The locks beeped and Pointer slid open the rear passenger door and helped Basset in. "I'll sit at the front," he said. "Thanks for meeting us so promptly, Mr. Bryson. And sorry it's so late."

"No worries. We're getting quite used to it, Inspector. Between us, we've nabbed a fair number of British ne'er-do-wells attempting to hide out here."

Pointer buckled up. "Long may the cooperation continue."

Bryson switched on the engine and pulled out into the flow of yellow and black taxis and private vehicles. "You've got a meeting with the police at ten tomorrow morning."

"Sergeant Basset will attend in my stead," Pointer said.

"Oh?"

Hugging his briefcase to his chest, Pointer said, "For reasons I won't go into now, I have to be careful about going out in daylight."

"Really?" Bryson glanced up at his rear-view mirror, eyeing Basset. "Sergeant. How's your Spanish?"

"GCSE basic, sir. I would hope we can get by, though."

Bryson smiled at her. "An interpreter will be provided by the embassy, in case. Oh, I've been in touch with the police about your two subjects of interest and was told that some hotels wouldn't pass on their new clients' details until tomorrow."

Pointer nodded. "That's to be expected."

"What about those with a direct link to the police computer?" Basset asked.

"They were very thorough and helpful and made a hasty check on the computerized information streamed in so far but it doesn't reveal anyone answering the name of Barnes or Gledhill registering in a hotel in the city."

"Let's hope their passport details show up tomorrow, then." Basset sat back. "Otherwise, we're going to hit a dead end before we start!"

Pointer half-turned in his seat and said, over his shoulder, "What happened to my positive sergeant, Sergeant?"

"All of a sudden, I'm stressed, sir. I remember getting confused over *estar* and *ser*... To be or not to be, that's the question!" She shuddered. "And don't get me on about all those nouns with gender..."

THEY CERTAINLY HADN'T HAD time to change. Leon took them to an intimate late-night restaurant with a jazz trio playing in the background. Cat ordered *pollo al ajillo* as she didn't want anything too adventurous on her first night. Grilled chicken with garlic sounded just fine.

Leon selected *pastel de carne*: "A favorite. I acquired the taste from Iran. It's a Murcian pie." It looked tasty—minced meat and chopped boiled eggs in a puff pastry case. But Cat felt it would be too filling this late at night.

Rick settled for a Catalan salad of vegetables, cured meat, and cheese.

They shared a bottle of Torres' red wine, *Sangre de toro*.

Cat voiced her concerns. "I know I feel I'm in the right to do all I can to hurt Dante and destroy Ananke but perhaps I'm being too harsh."

"Harsh?" Leon said. "In what way? You haven't physically hurt anyone, have you?"

"No. Any physical stuff has come from his people." She shivered at the memory of that man, Jenkins, brandishing the acetylene torch. "There are the company's employees' livelihoods to consider. I must assume that not all his workers are aware of his illegal business operations."

"If the money's good enough," Rick said, "they'll probably just turn and look the other way."

"I was careful when I started the fire in Angers. Nobody was hurt. I checked afterward."

"You've actually hurt the insurance company," Rick suggested.

Leon leaned forward on the table. "I don't know if Dante and his minions would show as much compunction about hurting you, Cathy."

She said, "I suppose you have a point there."

Leon said, "You have a conscience, Cathy. Remember that you have to live with your actions. If you bear that in mind, I suspect you'll find the right way."

"I hope so. I want to be a catalyst for change. A catalyst for justice."

Later, Leon settled the check and left them with the words, *"Buenas noches."*

ZABALA TRAWLED THE BARS. He knew what he wanted. She had to be exactly right. His blood was up and he needed for it to happen tonight. He'd switched off his cellphone after the first unanswered call from Petra. He didn't want to go near her when he felt like this. No telling what he would do in that case.

Sure, he knew she wanted him. But for her own wellbeing, she'd have to wait.

The Absinthe Bar was a regular haunt. It had been around for almost two hundred years and he felt at home with the dusty, old-fashioned decor, the cobwebs in the corners, and dingy, dim chandeliers. A barman once told him that Picasso and Hemmingway used to be regulars; not that he cared.

Plenty of young people frequented here, sometimes as a starting place before going on elsewhere. A few couldn't control their intake and took a hit too many.

He found a suitable woman nursing an absinthe with three empty glasses lined up in front of her at the end of the bar. She smiled with her mouth, but her dark eyes were without emotion. Yes, she would do nicely.

Chapter 12

Catananche

Cat was glad it was only a short walk back to the apartment block as she felt quite tired. She held Rick's hand, and it seemed the most natural thing to do.

The night air was warm, the odors from the restaurant lingering still in her nostrils, intoxicating. Citrus smells hovered from the orange trees that lined the road.

Despite the lateness of the hour, groups of youths, many dressed in smart clothes and bright colors, passed by, some talking loudly on cellphones. An occasional couple strolled with a child in a pram. They didn't encounter any drunks or rowdy elements. She felt surprisingly safe.

So many things told her this was an exotic country. It had always made her blood sing. Now, as she held Rick's hand, Spain seemed to possess more potential for excitement than she'd ever experienced. She smiled to herself. Excitement? Since meeting Rick, she'd had more than her fair share of that—and it nearly got them both killed in Wales!

Rick opened the door to the apartment and suddenly his mood altered. "We've had a long day. Was it just this morning we had breakfast on the M54?"

She said sleepily, "Yesterday morning. We've entered a new day."

"So we have." Gently, he led her to her bedroom and opened the door. "Good night, Cathy. Sleep tight." He shut the door.

For a moment or two, she stood there, feeling strangely bereft. A part of her wanted his company, his closeness.

She didn't remember undressing and climbing into bed.

Later that morning, she awoke feeling refreshed. She stretched under the sheet and glanced at the pillow beside hers. She recalled that time, in Bamburgh, waking to find him beside her, fully clothed, and there was a catch in her throat. That had been a good feeling.

Even as she showered, she kept thinking about him.

Over the meal last night, Leon had outlined what he had arranged so she decided to dress appropriately. In her suitcase was a mixture of designer and High Street garments. Intent on making an impression as a businesswoman, she put on her Janet Reger noir plum lace trim tulip bra, matching hipster briefs, a Madeleine light taupe trouser suit with a maroon silk blouson style shirt, and SJP 3.5-inch heels.

When she stepped out into the lounge, her heart jumped a little at the sight of Rick. It tended to do that, she noticed now. Her throat momentarily felt constricted.

"*Buenos días*," he said and grinned warmly. He wore an elegantly cut Armani single-breasted suit with a taupe hue. His shirt was cream, his tie brown. He laughed good-humouredly. "Taupe touché!"

She beamed and wondered if he wore Michael Kors briefs; tantalizingly, that image of him still lingered.

"Leon phoned," he said. "He's waiting for us at this address." He showed her a scribbled note. "It's what he calls a safe house with an 'interesting view'. He expects us in half an hour."

"Time for breakfast, then?"

"Definitely."

THE SAFE HOUSE room was stark and empty save for a pinewood table and four chairs. On the table was a black attaché case. From this window vantage point, Cat had a view of the buildings opposite. Unlike much of the architecture in the city, the block was unimpressive, resembling Soviet Utilitarian rather than Spanish gothic. In two places, the building was inset as if to allow for the very tall date palm trees that grew there; windows looked out onto the tree trunk while the palm fronds swayed above the rooftop. She'd seen this kind of thing before; it was as if the contractors had built around the trees. Maybe the fact that palms were protected had something to do with it? She noticed that the ground floor was a string of closed premises, the metal shutters marred by graffiti, an ancient curse of modern Spain.

Leon leaned a broad shoulder against the wall on

the left of the window. "Two years ago, Ananke took over that entire block of apartments."

"I joined Ananke on the tail end of the transaction," Rick said. "It was all but signed and sealed." He pointed. "The shops on the ground floor were bought out and shut, as you can see. I thought it drastic at the time, but I was new and couldn't question it."

"No signboards or notices," Cat observed, "just like the mine in Wales..."

Leon pushed himself off the wall. "So," Leon mused, "I suspect they're doing something illegal."

Rick nodded. "They're fair game, then."

Turning to face Rick, Leon held him by the arms and studied his face. "Be careful, my friend. This is no game. These people play for keeps."

Rick smiled sheepishly and massaged his head. The skin on his temple had scabbed over. "I know. It was simply a manner of speaking."

"I've got a man on the inside," Leon said, "but he only has clearance for the ground floor. He reports infrequent deliveries and departures of people at all hours of the day in a closed van."

"Is your man there now?"

"No. I told him to keep away today. I'll get the badges and we can start right away."

"No, Leon, you've done enough," Cat said. "We'll take it from here."

Leon frowned. "We?" He raised an eyebrow at Cat. "You're not going, surely?"

"I surely am."

His face clouded and Leon eyed Rick.

"Don't look at me like that, Leon," Rick said, "I tried talking her out of it. But to be honest, the last time we went up against Ananke, she was the one who got us out in one piece. I'd be floating off the Welsh coast by now if Cathy hadn't acted when she did."

"We were lucky..." she said.

"Well...the badges will still work, as it happens." He strode over to the table and swung the attaché case around, clicked the locks open, and lifted the lid. He took out two clipboards. "Under the top sheet is a sketch map of the interior," he said and then lifted up two badges. "My contacts had to work fast to provide these." The names on the badges read Z. *González* and L. *Mestre.* "Ananke only uses initials, no gender insignia, so substituting you, Cathy, for me is not a problem. How's your Spanish?"

"Fluent." She fixed the González badge to her lapel. "I was brought up in France, and my father and I traveled to Spain frequently."

"Good."

She looked at Rick. "And you?"

He pinned the other badge to his jacket. "Perhaps not fluent but, since I studied Latin, I found French and Spanish straightforward. I'll speak in monosyllables if it looks tricky—unless?"

"I can do the talking," she offered, "if necessary. Bear in mind, they might use Catalan, not Castilian, so there are differences."

"Oh, yeah, of course. Great..."

CAROL BASSET's prediction about a dead end proved to be accurate, Pointer mused. He paced in the hotel room, occasionally glaring out the window at the sunlight percolating through the palm leaves, creating long shadows. The noisy traffic of the city declared that it was busy already.

"If they leave the country through France," Basset said, "we're sunk."

Pointer stopped pacing and thrust his hands in his trouser pockets. "That's what comes of open borders. It doesn't help policing."

Bryson stood, walked over to the sideboard and poured a coffee. "It's a bit complicated. And difficult to administer."

"That's one reason why the UK never signed the Schengen agreement!" Pointer snapped. If traveling from one border-free Schengen country to another, EU nationals were not required to show a passport or a national ID card. UK wasn't the only country to opt out of this: Bulgaria, Croatia, Cyprus, Ireland, and Romania weren't part of the Schengen area either. "Spain to France—they won't show their passports, and nobody will challenge them, I bet!"

"Even though they should show them?" Basset ventured.

Pointer let out a laugh. "If you were up to no good, would you?"

"No, I thought the border controls would at least make an effort—channel people through different entry points, like you do in customs."

"Which seems to rely on people's honesty," Pointer said with a snort.

"Some people look guilty, though, don't they?" Bryson chimed in.

Basset smiled. "Yes, even the innocent travelers."

"Mr. Bryson, can the police keep a lookout?" Pointer asked.

"Yes, they've said as much. Maybe we'll get a lucky break."

"In the meantime, what's the news from Barnes's and Gledhill's credit card providers? Are they going to play ball with us?"

Basset shrugged her shoulders. "I'm still waiting on a response, sir."

Pointer resumed his pacing.

IT WAS ALREADY a hot day as Leon escorted them to an entrance porch on the side of the Ananke block. Both Cat and Rick carried their clipboards. On the left of the door was a metal keypad, a series of buttons, and a speaker grill. "My man gave me the combination. Six Five Four Eight."

Cat tucked her clipboard under her arm and pressed the keypad numbers.

In response, the door clicked open.

"You could have used the main entrance, but it will look better if you approach reception from the side door. The girl on duty will immediately consider you one of theirs since you got in with the combination."

"Okay," Cat said, "let's do it."

Leon sighed. "I wish I'd had the foresight to get a third badge made."

"Don't worry, we'll be fine," Rick reassured him. "Here, you better safeguard my little green book. Give it to me when we get back." Then, he stepped inside. He held out a hand to Cat. "Coming?"

She winked at Leon, grabbed Rick's hand, and, without a word, slid inside; even here, in a deserted corridor, the air-conditioning hit her with its welcome coolness.

Rick shut the door on Leon Cazador.

Strange, how that simple action, cutting them off from him, seemed to leave her slightly wanting. He had such a robust presence. Maybe it was charisma, something that Loup lacked. "Leon says the reception desk is through there." The short corridor led to an opaque glass door. "From now on, we speak in Spanish, all right?"

"Sure—I mean, *sí*..."

Cat and Rick walked warily along the short corridor and then tried the door handle. It turned and they entered a spacious atrium in silver and green with several colorful plants in large tubs. On the opposite side was a desk and seated behind it was a woman; on the wall behind her, large lettering announced *ANANKE, tu futuro ahora*. Your future now.

The receptionist stood as they approached; she wore a white blouse and black skirt; her badge declared she was *I^a. Blanco*: 'I^a' for Inma, a common name, Cat guessed, short for Inmaculada, after the immaculate conception of the Virgin Mary. No sign of a wedding band.

Senorita Blanco squinted at their badges and seemed satisfied by her scrutiny. "How can I help you?"

"Aren't you expecting us?" Cat queried forcibly.

Suddenly flustered, Señorita Blanco stammered, "N-no, there m-must be—must be a mix-up." She forced a smile and bobbed her head. "It happens too—too often..."

"I'm sorry to hear that. Señor Mestre and I have been assigned to validate the entire Ananke process for Catananche. We—"

"Cat—Catananche? Señora González, what is that?"

I wish I knew! Cat gave her a smile. "Ah, good, you do not know?"

Señorita Blanco shook her head, her dark eyes wide, worry reflected in them. "Should—should I know?"

"No. That is good." Cat made a hasty note on a sheet on her clipboard. "That bodes well for our inspection. There is no need for you to know anything about Catananche." She smiled lightly. "Pretend you have not heard it mentioned."

"Willingly, Señora González." She smoothed her skirt and produced a ledger from a shelf behind the counter. "Security requires that you complete your entry in my log."

"Good, very good." Cat used her own pen and scrawled Z. *González* on a line in the book, noting who the previous two entrants were this morning—Dr. Altozano and Prof. Quesada. She handed the pen to Rick. "Sign here, Señor Mestre."

Rick obliged, scrawling an approximation of his false name.

Cat retrieved her pen, slid it into her clipboard, and absently referred to the sketch under the board's clip. "I wish to go to the viewing room first." *El salón para observadores.*

"Ah, it is on the third floor." Señorita Blanco pointed to the two elevators and raised her phone handset to her ear. "I will call them so they will expect you."

Holding up a hand, Cat said, "No, Señorita Blanco, please don't do that. The nature of our visit requires that we appear unannounced. Only Señor Dante is aware of our business here."

Flustered again, this time at the mention of Dante, Señorita Blanco dipped her head. "Of course, whatever you say."

Cat and Rick strode purposefully to the elevator doors. "Have you done this kind of thing before?" he whispered in English when out of earshot.

"A couple of times. Most recently, in Angers. I imagine I'd have more difficulty getting into the head office of Harrods than I have in infiltrating any Ananke establishment." She tapped a finger on the red fire extinguisher fixed to the wall on the left of the right-hand elevator door. A plaque above it read *Extintor de CO2*. She thumbed at the sprinklers in the ceiling. "Their safety system may be okay but their security is almost a joke."

"Almost?"

"They have the occasional safeguard. Little traps, if you like. So far, I've been lucky and spotted them."

"So far?"

She grinned and pressed the elevator button. "Don't talk in the elevator. It might be bugged."

"Trusting soul, Dante, isn't he?"

"You should know, Rick. He trusted you to shadow me, didn't he?"

"Ouch, that hurt."

Through gritted teeth, she whispered, "Spanish, remember?"

"Ah, *sí, sí*..."

The elevator arrived and the doors opened. They

stepped into the spacious cubicle; it was big enough to accommodate a trolley. The doors glided shut and Cat pressed the number 3 button.

ZABALA STOOD NAKED, trembling with the aftershock of the murder. Slowly, determinedly, he came down from the high and glanced around. The dead woman lay on the bed, face up, no longer exciting him. Her black hair spread out on the pillow, forming a dark starburst around her head. Empty eyes stared at the ceiling. He almost felt sorry for her. Almost.

He padded to the bathroom and turned on the shower. While it ran, the hot water creating steam, he stepped out again. He wrapped the woman in the bedsheets and carried her to the shower cubicle then poured her out of the linen. She flopped and thudded against the tiled walls.

Slowly, almost lovingly, he used a nail brush and washed her, scouring all the blood and any tell-tale fibers from her. He found a packet of detergent in the cupboard under the basin and washed the sheet in the footwell of the shower. He had no intention of cleaning away the bloodstains; he merely had to contaminate any potential traces.

Still wet, he left his victim in the shower and went out into the bedroom. He retrieved his clothing from the chair, stood by the door, and slowly, methodically, dressed; the clothing clung to his wet skin. He sat on the bed and dried his feet with a towel and then carefully scanned the room. He was convinced he'd left no discernible trace. The concierge hadn't asked any questions when he'd arrived with the woman. It was that kind of hotel.

He got out by the rear emergency exit and breathed in the fetid air of the alley. One of these days, he would slip up, he felt sure. Perhaps the risk of discovery helped send the pulse racing?

Fortunately, he didn't need to sate himself so dramatically too often. As he crossed the road, sensing his body already drying in the morning heat, he wondered about Petra. He wouldn't want her to fall victim to his urges. That really would be a waste.

They seemed a good match together.

If I can arrange it, we'll enjoy a little pleasure cruise in the Med, courtesy of Dante. The emphasis on "pleasure", of course. Perhaps a little pain—but, now he was satisfied, not a fatal amount of pain.

Yes, I must be careful with Petra. She's good for me.

He decided that, after a bite to eat, he'd meet up with her, as agreed.

As CAT and Rick emerged from the elevator, a sign on the opposite wall indicated *el salon de CCTV* to the right, *dormitorios* to the left. Opposite the elevator doors, a single large window was set in the wall, offering the view of an exceedingly tall palm tree mere feet away and, beyond that, the city's rooftops. Across the road was the so-called safe house they'd been in earlier, the sun glinting on the windows, blanking out any activity. She wondered if Leon was watching from there.

They turned right.

A short way along the tiled corridor, they passed a

door marked *recreación* and then stopped outside the
door marked *el salon de CCTV*.

"Let me do the talking," Cat whispered in English
and opened the door.

Inside sat two men and a woman at a long bench
filled with eight CCTV terminals. It seemed that there
was movement in four separate rooms which were
currently under surveillance; two other rooms appeared
empty, and two screens were blank.

Dark-haired and thickset, the woman turned in her
chair and queried in a deep voice, "What are you doing
here? This is—"

"This is an impromptu inspection." Cat flashed her
fake pass and badge. "All of you are to remove yourselves from the room. I will give you further instructions
shortly. Wait in the recreation area."

The man on the left said, "But, security, Señor
Zabala is—"

"Señor Mestre here is security today," Cat said
firmly. "Just do as I tell you."

The three of them rose from their swivel chairs,
glanced at each other, and then shrugged. "I could do
with a smoke, anyway," said the woman.

Cat stood by the door and closed it after them.

"My God," Rick said in English, his voice hushed,
"I've heard of voyeurism, but this takes it all to a new
level!"

Crossing over to the bank of screens that Rick
was viewing, Cat studied one after another. The
screens of the four occupied rooms were marked A,
B, C, and D. Each screen showed two men and two
women, all naked and copulating in a frenzied
manner.

Some kind of metal discs were fixed to their foreheads; possibly remote monitoring terminals.

She was shocked to note that the bare backs of all of them were marred with red stripes, faint welts, as if they'd been flogged.

The rooms were sparsely furnished, each with a king-size bed, a wash basin, and a bidet.

Cat averted her eyes and then noticed the clipboards on the counter in front of each screen. There were lists; it seemed six men and six women were assigned to each room at certain times. The names of the individuals indicated that the majority were Eastern European, with a scattering of Asian.

"This can't be their clinical trials, surely?" she mused.

Rick clicked on the two blank screens and let out a gasp. "Oh, my God, look at them, Cathy." His tone seemed subdued. "Just look..."

Two rooms, slightly bigger than those with the beds, were crammed with people: one filled with women, the other with men. The people were in stained smocks, similar to those worn by patients in hospital, with bare buttocks in evidence.

"Cathy, look at their eyes."

She did and felt quite sick. "They seem drained, without any kind of will..."

"They're kept docile, I suppose. Until they have to perform in those bedrooms..."

"What the hell is that drug?" she whispered. "Some kind of aphrodisiac? It ties in with the name. Catananche caerulea—*Cupid's Dart* perennial... It was used by the ancient Greeks in love potions."

"Love potion's not the right name for *this*," he said,

grimly. "There's no love involved here." He fished out his cellphone. "I reckon it's time we called in the police." He gestured at the screens. "I bet they're all illegal immigrants."

Cat shuddered. "Forced into being guinea pigs for Ananke."

A chuckle at the door alerted her. Cat swung around.

A tall woman in a knee-length white lab coat stood holding the door open, one arm behind her back; her badge read: *Prof. Quesada.* Her black hair was bunched up high on her head and she wore black fishnet tights and black leather high-heeled shoes.

Standing at her shoulder was a short gray-haired man, slight of frame, with flinty eyes behind wire spectacles; his badge read: *Dr. Altozano.*

"They start out unwilling," Profesora Quesada said in English, her painted lips briefly curving in a thin smile, "but they soon crave for more, I assure you both."

"I find that hard to believe." Rick held up his phone. "Anyway, we'll soon see. When the police get here." He started to press the keypad when suddenly a whip lashed out and snatched the phone from his hand and it clattered to the tiled floor. He winced and moved back a step, hissing in pain.

Quesada flicked the whip on the floor. "I mastered this with my horses. They quickly learned to be docile. Our patients," She pointed the stock of her whip at the screens, "well, in time, they too came to appreciate the discipline of the lash."

"You can't treat people like this!" Cat stormed.

"You're not above the law!" Rick added, still nursing his hand.

Emitting a throaty chuckle, Quesada said, "You're hypocrites, aren't you? Entering these private premises without permission, eh?"

"We have right on our side!" Cat retorted.

"You're so naive, the pair of you. Many corporations are above the law these days. They're too powerful, too influential. Ananke is growing every day, spreading across the globe, and I'm proud to be a part of it."

"You won't get away with this," Rick seethed.

"That's so predictable and not very pithy," said a familiar voice.

Dr. Altozano moved aside, and Emilio Zabala entered, pointing an automatic pistol.

Chapter 13

"Fit for what?"

C at felt her stomach lurch as if she'd been punched there. She wanted to be sick but, instead, breathed in deeply and calmed herself.

Zabala's lips curved. "I'm distressed to see you're still alive, Mr. Barnes."

"You know this man?" Quesada demanded.

"Yes. He was Ananke's company lawyer."

"*Was?*" she queried.

"I revoked his contract when I left him for dead in Wales." Zabala pointed to their badges. "Who did you get those off? And how'd you get in? The combination code is changed every month."

Rick shrugged. "You have a few disgruntled ex-employees, perhaps?"

Swiftly, Zabala rushed forward and whipped the gun butt against the side of Rick's head. Rick grunted and stumbled against the terminal counter. The old wound opened up and seeped blood.

The sudden violence shocked Cat and she let out a gasp.

Rick steadied himself and raised a hand to his forehead.

Cat wanted to go to him, but she was held back by the strong grip of the doctor's hands on her arms.

"We're not in your British courts, Barnes," snarled Zabala. "My law applies here!"

Rick narrowed his eyes. "Yes, the law of the jungle, you big ape!"

Zabala raised his gun again, but Dr. Altozano stopped him. "What do you want to do with them, Señor?"

Zabala lowered his arm and eyed the bank of screens. "I see the latest activities are almost completed." He smirked. "Empty room C, Doctor."

Dr. Altozano let go of Cat's arms and moved to the counter, flicked a switch on the side of the screen, and spoke into a microphone. An eerie high-pitched sound emanated from hidden speakers. Abruptly, the cavorting couples desisted and sat up, staring into space. "You have fulfilled your task for now. Please leave the room in an orderly manner."

Docilely, the men and women, now seemingly oblivious of each other, gathered up their discarded smocks and walked out of the room.

"Take off your clothes," Zabala ordered, waving his gun.

"What?" Cat croaked.

"You can keep your underwear on. I want to be sure you're not carrying any weapon or another cellphone." He leered. "As a model, you shouldn't be concerned about flaunting yourself, surely?"

Cat didn't reply and took off her jacket, draped it on the back of a chair, and followed with removing her shirt. She flushed, despite herself. She sensed the lascivious eyes on her. There was something creepy, quite uncomfortable, about undressing in the presence of strangers, men who might do her harm. This was totally unlike all the times in changing rooms at fashion shows and photo studios. She kicked off her shoes and slipped out of her trousers. Out of the corner of her eye, she saw Rick undressing too, putting his clothing in a neat pile on another chair. Standing only in his Michael Kors briefs, he seemed as unnerved as she felt.

"A delightful twosome," observed Quesada. "You both appear quite fit."

"Fit for what?" Cat asked.

Zabala's lips curved, and he waved his gun. "You'll see. Now, let's go, the both of you. Lead the way, Doctor. Room C."

STANDING outside the Ananke building with Petra Grimalkin, Loup Dante slid his keycard into the portal. The doors soundlessly slid open. "Well, Petra, where is he?" he barked.

"I'm sorry, sir, but I can't locate Señor Zabala." Petra pocketed her cellphone and bit her lip. He was supposed to meet her here, damn him. It was all arranged, the pair of them would "borrow" Dante's yacht and spend a week sailing the Mediterranean, appeasing their lust and acquiring a deeper tan.

"I'm not pleased, Petra. Zabala should know better!"

"I agree, sir."

The pair strode through the main entrance and walked up to the reception desk.

Señorita Blanco stood up and beamed. "Your two inspectors are already here, sir, I sent them to—"

"Inspectors?" he demanded. "What inspectors?"

Blanco's face paled. She lifted the reception book and swung it around to face her boss. "Señora González and Señor Mestre."

"I've never heard of them!"

Petra rested a hand on Blanco's. "Where did you say you sent them, Señorita Blanco?" she asked gently.

"The viewing room..."

"The salon—?"

"Quick," Dante snapped, "we haven't a moment to lose!" He strode toward the elevator doors; Petra hurried behind him.

By the time the elevator arrived, she was by his side. "You think it's the Gledhill woman again?"

"It could be. Damn him, where's Zabala? I don't want another establishment razed to the ground!"

―――――――――

AT THE DOORS, Dr. Altozano pressed the button to summon the elevator. It arrived within a few seconds and they stepped inside. Even with the five of them, there was plenty of room in the car. Altozano selected the fourth floor. Nobody spoke. Cat noticed, out of the corner of her eye, that Zabala never lifted his gaze from her, intent on her chest. She shifted uncomfortably under his scrutiny and brushed against the bare torso of Rick. It seemed a very long time since they'd been this intimate. She flushed but not with passion, rather with anger. Her obsession had yet again thrust them both into mortal danger.

Thankfully, the journey was over quickly.

Exiting the elevator, they moved to the right and walked along the corridor. Her bare feet padding on the cool tiled floor, Cat felt vulnerable and at a disadvantage, almost naked next to her fully clothed captors. She imagined that Rick might feel even worse. At least, she was used to wearing next to nothing on the catwalk.

After blessedly few paces, they came to a door stenciled with a C.

The doctor opened the door, ushered them all inside, then closed it behind them.

Cat's mouth felt dry, and her gut clenched. She recognized the room all right: the disordered bedclothes; somebody hadn't retrieved their smock. She glanced up. They made no secret of the viewing camera.

"Our subjects are completely unaware of the camera, my dear," Quesada observed. "They crave only one thing—sexual gratification."

"Why have you brought us here?" Cat asked, fearing the answer.

Quesada chuckled. Cat hated that sound already. "The dosage we administer to our subjects is controlled, naturally, so we can monitor and gauge the effects. However, in your case, the both of you will be given quadruple dosage." She eyed Rick and ran her tongue over her lips. "I think when the drug takes hold of you both it really will be something to watch." Her eyes glinted in amusement. "You will literally tear each other apart, seeking to excite the pain-pleasure centers of your brains."

"I knew my studies in brain, biology, and behavior would come in useful one day," Cat quipped. Hollow words, she knew, but at least she was gratified that she had wiped the smirk from Quesada's face.

"That was a particularly brainless comment!" Quesada turned to the doctor. "Bring me the catananche, please."

"At once, Profesora." He left the room.

Rick shifted on his feet.

Zabala growled, "Don't move unless I say so, Barnes!" Then, he asked Quesada, "How long does it take for the drug to work?"

"Twenty to thirty minutes." Quesada rubbed a finger over her lips, licking it. "It might be sooner with the dosage increase..."

"Haven't you administered quadruple dosage before, then?" Cat asked.

"Oh, yes, and it always gives us the same result—as I've described. Naturally, the body-mass index will affect the speed of assimilation."

"You'll never get this past the EMA," Cat said.

Quesada cracked her whip on the tiled floor which made Cat jump involuntarily. "We almost have. Some of the so-called safeguards are not particularly efficient, shall we say?"

"Why peddle a dangerous drug?" Cat demanded. "You'll be shut down as soon as—"

"A drug that is approved is said to be 'safe and effective when used as directed'," Quesada countered. "Any aberrations will be the fault of those who misuse the drug. You're only a model so you won't know..." She gave another ghastly chuckle. "Then again, you models have a reputation as users of recreational drugs."

Quesada strode up to Rick and ran her whip's stock over Rick's bare torso. He flinched at the first touch but didn't react otherwise. Quesada tapped the stock against Rick's briefs and murmured throatily, "Viagra— or sildenafil as it's known—is mixed with illegal drugs, such as ecstasy and other stimulants or opiates, in an attempt to compensate for the common side effect of erectile dysfunction, a combination known as 'sextasy' or 'rockin' and rollin'."

"I'm aware of that," Cat said. "Mixing it with amyl nitrite's even more dangerous, even fatal..."

Pivoting around, Quesada pouted. She approached and brushed the stock of the whip against Cat's cheek. "I *am* impressed. Learn that from some of your model pals, did you? All experimenting to relieve the ennui of waiting to strut their stuff on the runway?"

Cat wasn't going to get into a discussion about the morals of her fellow models, many of whom were hard-working women tarred with the same brush as a few controversial sybarites. "This drug—catananche. I assume it's based on catananche caerulea—*Cupid's Dart* perennial. It was used by the ancient Greeks in love potions, wasn't it?"

"You do really impress me, my dear. Yes, it's combined with a special chemical concoction I've developed." Her left hand probed in her deep lab coat pocket and held up a memory stick. "It's all on here. I keep it with me at all times. And soon it will be ready for the public."

"EMA permitting."

"Oh, I assure you, they will permit it. Catananche is

the big money-spinner. It's going to be marketed as an aphrodisiac, bigger than Viagra because it homes in on the pleasure center of the brain, both male *and* female."

Dr. Altozano returned, pushing a small trolley that jostled metal implements and containers; one of its wheels squeaked.

Cat licked her lips and glanced left and right. Zabala watched her. No, he drooled at her. His gun was leveled at her navel. She wasn't going anywhere soon, it seemed—except to hell via insane ecstasy. Rick stood with clenched fists, his jaw set, lips tight, while his eyes threw ineffectual daggers at Profesora Quesada.

"Who will be first?" Zabala asked.

"The lady, I think," said Quesada.

"No!" Rick barked. "Inject me first. Let her go..."

Quesada laughed throatily. "How touching. He wants to save you." She shook her head. "No, the lady is first." She opened a long metal box and withdrew a hypodermic needle. The doctor handed her a vial and she inserted the needle in the top of the vial. Then, she slowly filled the hypodermic. "Hold her steady, please."

Dr. Altozano held Cat firmly by her upper arms.

"Watch her boyfriend, Señor Zabala."

"I've got him covered, Profesora."

"Good. That's it, Doctor, keep her steady." Quesada squirted the hypodermic to clear any air bubble.

Horribly mesmerized by the needle, Cathy heaved in a lungful of air, her chest straining.

Chapter 14

Dante

Breathless, Dante arrived in the CCTV room a few steps ahead of Petra and immediately noticed the clothing draped over the chairs. Then, he took in the scene presented on the monitor screen. His chest constricted at the sight of the Gledhill woman, about to be administered with an injection. The facial expressions of Zabala and Profesora Quesada told him plainly what they intended. "No!" he snarled, hastily snapping on the microphone and speaker to room C.

"Stop that at once! Do you hear me, Profesora? Bring both those people here *now!*"

"But—?" Zabala began.

"Did you hear me? *I said now!*"

Dante paced the room while they waited. Petra kept out of his way.

An age later, the door opened and Zabala entered. "Señor Dante, my apologies," he said. "I only wished to—"

"You had no right!" Dante blustered. He jabbed a

217

finger at the Gledhill woman. "She is not to be harmed! By you or anyone else, understood?"

Cathy Gledhill's face held a puzzled look. God, she looked beautiful, he thought, and his heart somersaulted. "Get dressed," he snapped, "the pair of you!"

"Gladly," said the Gledhill woman. Barnes, damn his eyes, kept his silence.

Dante's stomach squirmed as he noticed Altozano and Zabala watching Gledhill put on her clothes. He seethed at their behavior but decided not to comment for now.

When they were fully dressed, he barked, "To my office—at once!"

It was a silent, charged procession that wended its way along the corridor. At least Cat felt more comfortable now that she was dressed again. She wasn't a prude, but she'd felt her skin crawl when Altozano and Zabala made no secret of their appraisal of her. Her stomach squirmed now as she wondered what Dante had in mind. What did he mean about nobody harming her? Yes, right, she agreed with that, but she wondered why she was suddenly so special. And her heart skipped a beat as she realized that Rick wasn't regarded in the same light.

The office was two doors further along from the CCTV room.

As they all entered, Cat noticed that there was only one entrance and only one other exit: the window opened onto the main street. If she could somehow get out that window, she might be able to scale down the face of the building. But she doubted if Rick would be able to follow. She bit her lip. No, she couldn't leave him behind. It didn't bear thinking about what Zabala would do to Rick in the event of her escape. And there was the professor's whip, too; she fondled that quite lovingly.

Cat halted behind a ladder-backed chair in front of a mahogany desk. Quesada stood on her right, the whip looped over her shoulder, while Rick stood on her left, flanked by the doctor and Zabala.

Loup Dante moved to the desk, sat behind it, and unlocked the left-hand drawer. "Some information has been brought to my attention by...an associate..." He scanned each of them in turn.

Both Zabala and Petra shifted their feet uncomfortably. Curious, Cat studied the doctor and the professor; neither medic seemed perturbed by Dante's comments. Rick inclined his head to one side, glaring up at the CEO of Ananke. *If looks could kill...*

Now, Dante opened the desk drawer and took out a large brown envelope.

Cat noticed that Zabala visibly relaxed; he eyed her, a smirk on his face.

Dante wafted the envelope about and then opened it, tipping the contents onto the inlaid surface of his desk.

Cat's breath caught in her throat. Spread out for all to see were the pages ripped from her photograph album, plus letters, and account sheets. Her memories, her financial details. Her mouth felt dry. Her fingernails dug into her palms as she clenched and unclenched her hands. She blinked in vain to prevent the tears from forming on her lids. Agitatedly, she wiped her eyes, glaring at Dante and then at Zabala.

Leveling his gaze on her, Dante said, "I now learn, Cathy Gledhill, that this is not your true name."

"Eh?" Rick raised his head and glanced across at her.

In a swift response, Zabala clamped a hand on Rick's arm and pressed his gun against Rick's neck.

Jerking his head to face Rick, Dante snapped, "You were taken in by her, were you? She takes after her mother, I think. Her real name is Catherine Vibrissae..." His eyes appeared moist. He glanced down at his hands, opened another drawer, and withdrew a photograph in a frame.

From where she stood, though, Cat couldn't see the photo.

He studied the picture for a long moment then lifted his chin and stared at her. "Your features take after Deborah, your mother." His voice croaked toward the end.

"Cathy," Rick said, "what's going on?"

Cat's eyes darted to Rick. "I'll explain in a while." She waved a hand to dismiss his concern and then addressed Dante: "How well did you know my mother?"

"Yes, *very* well, in fact." Dante stood up and turned the photograph around for her to view.

It was a portrait of her mother, all right. She'd seen one similar. Her mother stood beside a younger version of Loup Dante. The one she'd seen featured her mother and father, though, on one of those ripped-out album pages.

A hand affectionately stroking the picture, Dante

said, "Your mother and I enjoyed a brief—all too brief —affair."

Her legs felt weak; she was afraid they'd buckle under the sudden weight of this revelation. Her voice sounded thick, her mouth as arid as her heart now seemed. "I don't believe you."

"It's true."

"For a brief, so very brief time, we seemed to lose our way, my dear," her father had said.

"Your father found out, forgave her." Almost reverently, Dante lowered the picture to his desk, face down, as if to look at her any longer was too painful. "Some eight or so months afterward, you were born."

She reached out for support and held onto the chair back. "You can't mean—?"

"I most certainly do." He nodded. "I need to take a DNA sample, compare it with mine." He glanced over at Quesada. "How long will it take?"

The professor licked her lips. "I don't have the facilities here. But I have contacts. I can get the results to you in twenty-four hours."

"That will have to do, I suppose. Good."

Tears trickled over Cat's cheeks. Images from her past flickered in her mind's eye—her father, their holidays, and the fun they had together; all of that couldn't be a lie! She set her jaw, straightened up, and then relinquished the support of the chair, her hands clenched into fists at her sides. "If you're my father, I'm Darth Vader."

"I don't understand your allusion; who or what is Darth Vader?"

"Oh, never mind!"

Dante bit his lip and turned to Rick. "I'm disappointed in you, Mr. Barnes."

Rick shrugged. "I can live with that. Tell me, is that why you wanted me to follow her, because you think Cathy's your daughter? You wanted to spy on your daughter?"

"I wanted to keep her safe." Dante glanced briefly at Cathy then turned his ire back to Rick. "For some misguided reason, she seems intent on destroying my business! If it had been anyone else, she would have been *crushed*!" He slammed a fist into a palm.

Rick growled, "Like you crushed my brother-in-law, David Ambrose?"

Dante shook his head. "I do not know any David Ambrose."

Glaring at him, Rick shrugged off Zabala's grip. "Maybe Emilio here can enlighten you! David was killed at your Seahouses plastics plant and it was made to look like an accident!"

Laughter erupted from Dante and he gazed at the ceiling. "Oh, you have been watching too many American movies, Rick Barnes. Conspiracies jumping out at you, I shouldn't wonder!" He shook his head. "Señor Zabala is my head of security, nothing more."

"Then you'll let Cathy and me go, will you?"

"Ah, there lies my dilemma. If Cathy is my daughter, as I strongly believe, then I am sure I can rely on her familial loyalty." He paused, pursed his lips, and then grimaced, as though he'd had an instant thought that proved distasteful. "You, however, clearly have no loyalty toward me. That is a proven fact."

Zabala grabbed Rick's arm again. "I can reserve a grim fate for him, sir."

"What...?" Puzzlement creased Dante's face.

"Do you really want to know?"

"No," Dante said, eyeing Cathy, "perhaps not. Not here, not now."

"You're a callous hypocrite," Cathy seethed. "You're lying about Mr. Ambrose! You're lying about being my father, too! Why have you waited all this time to reveal this? Why didn't you come forward when Papa died?"

Dante's eyes lanced at her and his mouth moved, lips twisting. Whatever his answers were, he kept them to himself.

"Sir," interrupted Zabala, "is your yacht *Alzahra* still moored at Olimpic?"

"Yes!" Dante grated. "What of it?"

"I'd like to take Barnes for a little outing." Zabala's lips curved. "This time, I'll make sure there's no mistake about an accidental drowning..."

Cat felt faint, swayed, and wanted to shout "No!" but her mouth was so dry it was incapable of voicing even a whimper of concern for Rick. Her heart seemed to have plunged into a stomach that roiled as if in a tempest. She fought down the bile, her eyes beseeching Dante.

"I didn't want to know that..." Dante's eyes were evasive, and then he nodded. "But, yes, take *Alzahra*." He opened a drawer, picked up a small bunch of keys on a fob, and tossed them to Zabala. "Bring her back tomorrow, though. I was planning to sail the Mediterranean for a couple of weeks." He looked at Cathy; she turned her face away and avoided his eyes. "Now, I can take my long-lost daughter..."

"I will, sir." Zabala glanced at Petra Grimalkin; he dipped his head at her then smiled briefly.

At gunpoint, Zabala shoved Rick out the door.

Again, overwhelming emotion clenched Cat's ribcage, almost crushing, as the door shut on them. She wanted to rush out and chase after them, but Petra stood by the door, her eyes steely, cold.

A few seconds of tense silence passed. Then, Petra cleared her throat and said, "Sir, I'm needed downstairs."

Dante nodded. "Go on, then. There's nothing for you to do here."

"Right, sir." Petra opened the door, stepped out, and shut it behind her.

"What about this one, sir?" Quesada asked, jabbing the handle of her whip between Cat's shoulder blades.

"That depends on whether she's my flesh and blood or not..." Rising to his feet, Dante added, "We'll find out, shall we?" He strode over to a door on his left and opened it to reveal an en suite room, with a set of drawers, a washbasin, a shower cubicle, a bidet, and a lavatory. He rummaged in a drawer and pulled out a small plastic box of cotton buds and two tumblers. "Here, Profesora Quesada. Swab me, please."

"Yes, sir. Doctor, watch Miss Gledhill-Vibrissae."

Altozano's hand clamped on Cat's upper arm while Quesada looped the whip around her own neck, stepped forward, and took a bud.

Cat was tempted to employ her taekwondo skills, but there were three of them and then there was the professor's whip.

"Open wide." Quesada ran the bud end around the

inside of his cheek. She then placed it in one of the tumblers.

He picked up a felt tip pen and marked the glass "LD". "Now, Miss Vibrissae."

Cat felt Altozano's grip tighten. She wanted to struggle. Even taking a buccal smear seemed invasive right now. But she knew that they would persevere until they got what they wanted. Obligingly, she opened her mouth.

Paloma Picasso scent wafted up her nose as the professor firmly held her jaw and dabbed and twirled a second bud on the inside of her cheek; she then placed it in the other unmarked tumbler. "There, that wasn't so bad, was it?" she said.

Cat sensed an after-impression from the bud, but it would pass in a second or two. "You're wasting your time," she retorted.

"Actually," Quesada said, "in your case, we're killing time before we decide to feed you to some of my more rabid subjects."

A shiver scampered over her flesh. The woman wasn't joking. At least until the DNA test results came in, she was relatively safe: as long as there was a risk of her being Dante's child, his minions would hold back.

The professor picked up the two tumblers. "What shall I do with her while we wait on the test results, sir?"

"Keep her in a dormitory. Bring her to me with the results."

"Yes, sir."

But what will he do when he finds out that I'm not his daughter? He'll dispose of me, just as Zabala is about to do with Rick. Oh, God, Rick...

Chapter 15

Extinguished

Rick and Zabala walked out of the building and joined the milling crowds. A tram passed. For a fleeting second, Rick considered jumping onto the tram but its doors were shut so it wasn't possible. He was also acutely aware of the gun Zabala held in his jacket pocket.

Zabala didn't look out of place here; there were plenty of Spaniards strolling the sidewalk in their open-necked shirts and lightweight, colorful suits.

Would Zabala risk shooting in a busy street? Rick wasn't going to find out. Jenkins had been ruthless, quite willing to kill them both with the acetylene torch. He guessed Zabala was definitely just as bad.

"You are a wimp," Zabala whispered in his ear.

"I'd rather be a live wimp than a dead hero," Rick replied.

"Live for the moment, anyway," Zabala observed with a mocking snigger.

Rick felt nauseous, not only because of his grim predicament but, also, due to the worry about Cathy that gnawed at his vitals. He should have done something rather than leave her with Dante. His heart ached as he realized he might never see her again. He now had no illusions about the end that Zabala planned for him. The prospect of death made him sweat, but the loss of Cathy seemed even more devastating.

"Oh, by the way, you were right," Zabala said, breaking into his thoughts. "I did kill David Ambrose. I was pleased the way it turned out—'accidental death'."

Rick tensed but kept walking. He hated Zabala enough already. His suspicions being confirmed didn't alter that fact. Tamping down his hatred, he asked, "How far is it to the port?"

"A short walk. Mind how you go," he added as they crossed the busy road. "The trams, they seem to come out of nowhere." They dodged a taxi in the city's distinctive yellow and black livery. "And don't think of trying to get away. I won't hesitate to shoot. By the time anyone knows what has happened, you will be dead and I will have disappeared among the crowds."

QUESADA PRESSED the stock of her whip against Cat's back and shoved her out of Loup Dante's office. Dr. Altozano followed a pace behind, carrying the two tumblers with their respective cotton buds.

Chuckling throatily, Quesada rested the knob of the whip on Cat's shoulder as they walked along the corridor.

Even if she ran for it, Cat felt sure the whip would find her before she could reach the elevators. The thought of escaping in an elevator was academic, she realized as they reached the doors: it was evident that both elevators presently rested on the ground floor. Besides, if she'd made a break for it, the second elevator would follow.

Dr. Altozano jabbed the call button which lit up next to a fire extinguisher.

As they waited for the elevator to ascend, Quesada chuckled, the sound grating on Cat's nerves. "You know, I can't see you being loyal to Señor Dante even if you learn that he sired you."

Cat eyed her, raising an eyebrow. She wasn't going to respond; the woman was baiting her, she felt sure. It was in her vile nature.

Dr. Altozano said, "Profesora, what do you mean?"

Quesada smirked and looked askance at Cathy as she fingered the whip that she now looped around her neck. "Loup Dante arranged the death of Daniel Vibrissae."

Cat sucked in air, shock pummeling her, making it difficult to breathe. Words of protest formed in her head but didn't arrive at her lips. She felt cold, very cold. Goosebumps formed on her forearms. It could be a malicious lie, intended to hurt her; Cat wouldn't put it past the woman; she seemed to favor torturing her subjects as she called them. But Cat believed it. How did Dante manufacture the 'accident', though?

"Don't worry, my dear," Quesada said. "When you prove a disappointment to Dante and he discards you, I will make use of you as I promised. You will be an interesting subject in my trials. I suspect that you will exhibit great stamina."

Her emotions in sudden turmoil, Cat felt the blood deserting her head and she slumped forward, extending a hand to the wall beside the elevator doors. Next to the fire extinguisher.

"Oh, Miss Gledhill, have we upset you, is that it?" Quesada chuckled as she rested a hand on Cat's upper arm. "Poor soul!"

———

PETRA HURRIEDLY EXITED the elevator and made straight for her office next to the reception desk. Her pre-packed leather travel case leaned against the leg of her small desk. She grabbed it, wheeled it behind her, signed out, and left the building.

She was tempted to catch a tram, but they weren't that frequent and she couldn't bear standing, waiting.

Waiting. Yes, she knew he'd be waiting for her at the yacht; his eye contact told her that. It was smooth of him, to introduce the yacht into the equation using Barnes as an excuse.

She felt her cheeks glow warmly as she thought of witnessing the demise of Barnes out at sea. She'd never seen a man killed before. The very idea sent a frisson down her spine. She was sure that Zabala took pleasure in it. She pursed her lips; he certainly took pleasure in hurting women. That had been a surprise, too. She hadn't believed she could derive so much sensual gratification from experiencing pain.

Somebody nudged her elbow and jogged her out of her reverie. No apology. As she crossed the street, a woman got in her way. Petra pulled the case around her, the stupid cow, and was nearly run down by a taxi.

Damned crowds! The sun brought them out.

She took greater care now and wove through the passers-by.

Everybody seemed to be walking at an infuriatingly leisurely pace. Didn't anyone ever hurry to an appointment?

He'd wait for her, she knew.

THE FIRMNESS of the wall stabilized Cat and clarified her thoughts. "I'll be all right." In one swift, smooth movement, she snatched the extinguisher off its wall bracket, swung it around, and its base hit Quesada under the chin. "That'll wipe the grin off your face!"

Quesada stumbled sideways against the elevator doors. Her eyes seemed glazed. Blood dribbled from the corner of her mouth.

Dr. Altozano exclaimed and, in that same instant, Cat pulled off the plastic safety cover, extracted the pin, and sprayed him. The doctor dropped the two DNA sample tumblers and backed away, covering his face with his hands, coughing and sputtering. The tumblers shattered on the floor. Cat sprayed the cotton buds then released the lever, stopping the extinguisher's flow.

Standing the extinguisher upright, she slickly delved into Quesada's deep coat pocket and grabbed the memory stick. Then, on the spur of the moment, she tugged the whip from around the vile woman's neck.

Hardly breaking pace, she picked up the extinguisher again and slammed it into the fire alarm box on the wall, breaking the glass. She took the key, inserted it, and set off the alarm. That should bring the authorities, she thought, and they were bound to discover the immigrants.

As the alarm blared in her ears, with all her might, Cat flung the extinguisher at the big window and the window shattered into thousands of shards.

Cat leaped up and mounted the sill. For a moment, she tottered there while she glanced over her shoulder. One of the elevators had arrived, its doors sliding open. It was so tempting. But, even if she could get to the elevator, she'd never make it out the front door. Quesada was slumped against the doors of the other elevator, groggy, while the doctor was on his knees, hands searching for his spectacles.

Cat took off her SJP shoes and stuffed them down the front of her blouse then turned, looked out at the tall palm tree, and hastily gauged the distance.

She jumped across space.

Her body slammed into the tree trunk, and she felt the heels of her shoes dig into her midriff. She held on while her bare feet jammed into the husky, hard surface. Her hands gripped tightly onto the rough, quite prickly, and fibrous bole. She looped the whip around the trunk and grabbed the other end. Using it to support herself, she slowly descended, lowering one foot at a time, much in the manner of natives climbing to retrieve coconuts or dates, perhaps—though now she was in hasty reverse and gritted her teeth as the coarse fiber dug into the soles of her feet.

The fire alarm sound impinged on her consciousness.

Below, passers-by stared up, some pointing. As far as they were concerned, she would be escaping a fire.

She jumped the last few feet, landing firmly if a

little painfully on cut soles. She dug out her shoes and put them on. She folded the whip, shoved it under her arm and, trying not to limp, she marched purposefully away, through the milling crowd.

Nobody stopped her. Perhaps her stern face deterred any interference.

Before crossing the road, she peered over her shoulder. Doubtless, by now, onlookers would be wondering where the smoke was from the fire. She'd dearly have loved to set off the sprinkler system to ruin the computers but, in reality, they didn't work like they showed in movies. They have to be triggered by a strong heat source. The sprinkler heads must detect a high temperature between 57 to 74 degrees Celsius. The sprinkler head's equipped with a glass trigger filled with a glycerin-based liquid that expanded at the appropriate temperature, breaking the glass and activating the sprinkler. There was no way she could generate that kind of heat. Besides, sensibly, the sprinkler design would be localized. She'd have dowsed the corridor, nowhere else.

She limped across the road. While on the windowsill she'd worked out her bearings. Now, the port was directly ahead, at the bottom of this street. She must get to the marina, Port Olimpic. Police were bound to be there, surely, and they could help Rick.

DEAFENED by a terrible warning fire alarm sound, disoriented and swamped in pain, Quesada pushed herself upright against the elevator doors. She gritted her teeth, but that hurt, *dios mio*, did that hurt! Her jaw felt very sore, achingly sore, more than the rest of her body, though her shoulder and hip felt badly bruised, and there was a hole in her tights at the knee. For an instant, she forgot how it happened. Then she saw Dr. Altozano and remembered. The Gledhill woman!

"She's gone—and ruined the samples!" wailed Altozano, fumbling as he fitted on his spectacles; one of the lenses was cracked.

Some instinct or hazy memory made her check her pockets. She vaguely recalled someone leaning over her, even though she'd been groggy. She gasped as she realized the memory stick wasn't in her pocket. She winced. No, she wasn't concerned about the samples, but she was worried about her research getting into the wrong hands. Yes, it was backed up and on her hard drive, but that memory stick was important, vital to their project. It also happened to contain all the results from her subjects, in fine prurient detail.

Trembling with frustrated anger, she glared at the shattered window and the palm tree swaying outside. Surely Gledhill couldn't have gone out that way? She glanced at the elevator; its doors were open, jammed there by one of her shoes that had somehow become wedged between them. The other elevator was still at the ground floor.

Limping over, she retrieved her shoe, jabbed the elevator call button, and waited for the doors to fully open. At least the elevators were still operational. Some years ago she'd been caught in a hotel fire and all the elevators had been automatically sent to the ground floor for the emergency crews and set inoperable till they arrived.

The journey down seemed to last forever.

Finally emerging from the elevator in the foyer, she shouted to the receptionist, "Cancel the alarm. Tell the fire department it's a mistake!"

"But Señora, I—I..."

With a limping gait, she exited the foyer. But where to go?

Gledhill's companion, Barnes. It made sense. Zabala was taking Barnes to the marina. Gledhill would go there.

I must retrieve the memory stick!

She hastened as much as her pained limbs would allow, crossing the road, and ran over the tram tracks.

The T4 tram hit her broadside, slamming into her hip, shoulder, and head. Massive pain swamped her. She heard onlookers scream as the tram came to a halt, but the sounds grew faint and, then, oblivion engulfed her.

OBLIVIOUS TO RICK'S PREDICAMENT, people milled about Moll de Xaloc, where many of the motor and sailboats were moored. Looming above them were two forty-story buildings—the five-star Hotel Arts and the Mapfre Tower. Clearly, tourism and insurance pays; right now, he reckoned he was in the wrong business.

The *Alzahra* was bunched in among other yachts.

Zabala urged him up the short gangway onto the deck. Then he handcuffed Rick to the guardrail.

"Where'd you get these?" Rick asked. "Playing at rough sex?"

Sneering, Zabala said, "You forget, I'm head of security. I've got access to all the tools of my security operatives." Then he spun around and descended the gangway onto the marina's jetty. He strode along to the hawser at the bow, and then aft.

Within a few minutes, he'd cast off the yacht, got aboard, and pulled in the gangway. He hastened to the cockpit and started the motor.

Expertly, Zabala steered the boat slowly past the moored vessels, nudging the occasional fender.

He kept glancing over his shoulder, looking anxious.

His HEAD POUNDING with the insistent fire alarm, Dante exited the elevator and hurried across the entrance foyer to the reception desk. "Why is the alarm still on, Señorita Blanco? There is no fire!" He'd spoken to the dazed Dr. Altozano, leaving him at the elevator doors. He was furious that Catherine had escaped before the DNA tests could be set up. Yet, he harbored a sneaking respect for her audacity, too. *I should have pressed my case for fatherhood much earlier*, he reasoned.

"Señor, I know, the *profesora*, she says there is no fire but I cannot get in touch with the fire department. I haven't been trained to... I—I can't stop the alarm, Señor, *lo siento!*"

Petra was supposed to be here, wasn't she? "Where is—?" Then he heard a commotion and glanced through the double glass entrance doors and noticed a big crowd assembled outside.

Tentatively, he walked to the doors, opened one, and stepped onto the porch.

An ambulance had arrived promptly but the bystanders nearby all looked quite glum, some shaking their heads. The tram stood in its tracks, the driver sitting in his cab with his head in his hands.

Dante gently insinuated himself to the front of the crowd.

He recognized Profesora Quesada immediately.

At that moment, the fire department arrived.

He clenched his teeth until his jaw hurt. Somehow, he doubted that the fire chief would walk away without checking the building. They'd find Quesada's test subjects, of course, and the fallout would be horrendous. Better if the building *had* been on fire!

Dante pushed his way to the rear of the crowd where he glimpsed his reflection in a shop window. He looked haggard, shoulders slumped. Weary of life... Damn Catherine! Not so many minutes ago, he'd had grudging respect for her. But now, he hated her. Now, he wanted to be rid of her.

What, even if she's my daughter? What am I building an empire for, if not my heir? An heir I don't have—unless she is the one.

I will hound her, he decided. Hound her to the ends of the earth. She has already wounded me. More than once. Now, it will be *my* turn.

His reflection grinned back at him. No, he wasn't weary of life. Energized. He hadn't felt this good in a long time. Possibly not since he plotted the death of Daniel.

Time to call in a few favors, I think.

Where the hell is Zabala?

Then he remembered. He was due to return with the yacht tomorrow.

Considering everything that was likely to explode into the public eye from today's farce, I think it would be prudent if the yacht didn't dock here tomorrow. I'll contact him by radio and arrange a meeting somewhere else. Marseille or Nice, perhaps. Then, I will use Zabala's contacts and hunt down Catherine Vibrissae, Cathy Gledhill, or whatever she decides to call herself.

Dante rubbed his hands together in anticipation. During the hunt, she is bound to leave some trace, something we can use to verify the DNA. If she isn't my daughter, then Zabala can have the pleasure of dealing with her.

His heart turned but it was the only rational response he could make. If she is my daughter, only I will spill her blood. She won't be the heir to my fortune, only to my wrath. That is the satisfaction I will require.

Chapter 16

Becoming a Habit

P etra ran along the marina jetty, her follow-me case making a clattering noise. She'd sailed on Dante's yacht a couple of times but she'd been with the others and hadn't paid much attention to its mooring position.

Now, anxiously, she scanned the decks of the bobbing boats.

People kept obscuring her view. She moved forward and dodged a couple holding hands.

There! Emilio was already taking the boat out. Why didn't he wait?

Dragging the travel case behind her, she increased her pace. "Emilio, wait!" she wailed. "Please, wait for me!"

He was too far away to hear her. She raised a hand and waved frantically.

Her heart leaped as he spotted her and returned her wave.

The wake from the yacht settled. He'd stopped the engine.

He was waiting for her. Surely he'd motor back now.

Abruptly, she winced as something stung her cheek. She gasped and raised a hand to her face to ward off a wasp. Blood covered her fingers, and the pain was intense. It wasn't a sting but a lengthy cut.

"You're not going anywhere, Petra!"

She turned and stared in disbelief. The Gledhill woman was about six feet from her, wielding a whip. The bitch! That must be the profesora's whip! She touched her cut cheek again and trembled.

Thrusting aside her travel case, she ran along the jetty in the direction of the becalmed yacht.

Emilio was edging the boat inshore.

Now, she saw the lawyer, Barnes. He was hand-cuffed to the guardrail.

She wasn't fit, she realized, already gasping for breath. It wasn't meant to be like this! We're supposed to sneak off on a holiday jaunt—sun, sea, and sex. She held on to the fact that Emilio was coming back for her.

The whip snaked around her ankle in mid stride and she tumbled and fell, hitting her knee and palms on the stone flags. Her whole body seemed to jar with the sudden impact.

Seconds later, Gledhill was on top of her.

SEVERAL ONLOOKERS BACKED away as Cat leaped at Petra lying on the jetty. She landed softly, on the woman's torso, hopefully knocking the wind out of her.

Screaming, Petra lashed out with flailing fists and one connected, hitting Cat a glancing jolt on the chin.

It stung. She tried grabbing Petra's wrists, sustaining bruising blows to her forearms. She got hold of one wrist, yanked hard, and swiveled it, forcing Petra onto her side. Cat held tight and pushed Petra's arm up her back.

Petra swore and yelled and kicked her legs ineffectually.

Cat glanced up and noticed that the yacht was now much closer to the jetty but still several yards off.

A man walked up to her and asked in Spanish, "Excuse me, Ma'am, what's this all about?"

She replied, "It's a family issue. Please call the police at once!"

"*Sí, sí!*" He ran off, shouting to other onlookers to keep clear, he would get the police.

Ensuring her grip was firm, Cat regained her feet, dragging Petra up with her. She moved toward the edge of the jetty.

"Zabala!" she hollered. "Let Rick go and I'll give you Petra in exchange!"

Petra agitatedly nodded. "Please, Emilio, do as she says!"

Scowling, Zabala hesitated, his legs spread to steady himself on the deck as the swell of the water rocked the vessel. He eyed Rick, then the handful of people watching.

Cat gambled that he wouldn't dare bring out his gun.

"Very well!" Zabala shouted.

A joyous sensation spread through her but she didn't relinquish her hold on Petra.

Zabala fumbled at the guardrail and then pushed at Rick.

Cat's heart tumbled as, unbalancing over the rail, Rick fell head-first into the harbor water.

An instant later, he surfaced with a grin on his face.

Cat shoved Petra forward, to the edge of the jetty. Then she let go of Petra's arm and shoved her firmly.

Petra shrieked as she fell into the water. She went under and then broke the surface, sputtering. She swam toward the yacht, passing Rick on her way. Neither Rick nor Petra paused for a chat.

Seconds later, Cat helped Rick up onto the jetty, water cascading from his clothes.

She noticed that Petra was scaling the ladder at the stern of the yacht. Once she was onboard, the motor started and the vessel sailed toward the exit of the mole.

Cat laughed, hugging him, despite his drenched clothes. "Seems like this is becoming a habit, fishing you out of hot water."

"Who said it was hot?"

A few onlookers applauded them.

Sirens sounded, getting nearer.

"I think we'd all better take our leave," said Leon Cazador softly.

They both turned around in surprise.

"I followed you here, Cathy. You don't think I'd abandon you, surely?"

"No, but...oh, the police..."

Leon smiled. "It's all right. I know them. I'll explain it's a domestic situation. They won't want to get involved, particularly as nobody was hurt."

Glancing out to the receding yacht, Cat mused, "Oh, I wouldn't say that." She picked up the whip.

Mediterranean Sea

Petra stood on the stern of the yacht, absently fingering the whip-lash on her cheek. Emilio embraced her from behind and squeezed her. "What are you thinking?" he asked, breathing in her ear.

"I want to hurt the Gledhill woman. Very much."

Emilio Zabala leaned close, kissed her on the neck, and nibbled her ear. "I think, one day, we will get what we want, dearest."

She turned in his arms, lifted her face to his, and their lips crushed briefly, insistently.

The sea-to-shore radio blared for attention.

Reluctantly, Zabala disengaged and said, "Later. It seems our boss is calling sooner than I expected."

She let him go and touched her slightly bruised lips.

He descended the steps into the cabin area while her insides stirred in expectation of a night full of promise.

Still flushed with warm thoughts, she frowned when he emerged after barely a couple of minutes. "That was a short conversation."

He shrugged. "Dante has abandoned the catananche facility. He wants to meet us in Nice—the day after tomorrow."

"Oh." She was disappointed, having looked forward to at least a week at sea with Emilio.

"Don't worry. We can cram a lot into the time we have left on his yacht."

She perked up at that. "Promise?"

"Oh, yes, Petra." His thin lips curved in a lascivious grin, and he held up a set of handcuffs.

"Deal," she said. Her voice was husky with anticipation.

Chapter 17

Gut Feeling

Barcelona, Spain

"It's going to take a few days to arrange your fake passports," Leon said. "Spanish ones so that you comply with the requirements of the Schengen free border crossing in the EU."

"I was going to ask how you know people who can do that..." Rick said. "Stupid of me, I know."

"My colorful past has meant I've rubbed shoulders with all kinds of individuals. Many of them reside in a gray area, shall we say? Under the radar, off the net. Providing they don't tread in those areas that I'm actively against, then I'm happy for them to continue operating. I don't see any reason why only criminals should take advantage of them. Sometimes, the good guys need to travel incognito, yes?"

Cat smiled. "Yes. A definite 'yes', Leon."

His face took on that serious cast again. "Be sure that you tread with care. Dante now knows you're after him and, from what you've told me, he knows a great deal about you."

FINALLY, Cat and Rick read the story about the Seahouses plant when it broke in the UK press.

One comment ran, "It is ironic that a factory working on biodegradable plastics, which are designed to safeguard nature, should be responsible for such wanton pollution."

Another ran an apologist line from the Ananke lawyers: "Nobody deliberately designs a factory or any other facility with the intention of causing pollution. Unfortunately, sometimes in the design or planning stages, mistakes are made and the consequences are not appreciated until it is almost too late. Sometimes, shortcuts are taken or inferior products are used and the result is a systemic breakdown. Then, measures must be taken to limit the problem. Ananke has recognized that unauthorized action was taken that resulted in this unwanted, undesirable pollution. The plant will close immediately until the problem can be rectified. Those responsible will face stern disciplinary action."

Rick grinned. "I guess Len's man got the story out without Ananke blocking it."

"It seems so. Dante has been hurt in his pocket yet again. For now, that's enough."

Then, a few days later, reports appeared in the press—*El País, Información,* and *La Vanguardia*—about the illegal immigrants being tested in the catananche facility in Barcelona.

The dormitories had been locked but the shouting

of the immigrants had attracted the notice of the fire chief while he conducted an inspection. He discovered a canteen and ablutions area attached to the dormitories. The staff members didn't appear to realize that anything illegal was going on.

The authorities were unable to locate the business owner, Loup Dante. However, his lawyers issued a statement that certain staff in Barcelona had overstepped the mark and abused their positions. This was "an isolated case and had no bearing on his other concerns in Barcelona and elsewhere. Mr. Dante has authorized generous payments to those individuals subjected to such traumatic procedures, without prejudice, of course."

"Of course," Cat said, flinging down *El País*.

POINTER HELD up *El País* and shook it at Sergeant Basset. "I'm beginning to wonder if we may be chasing the wrong people!"

Basset screwed up her eyes. "I'm not with you, sir. Ananke seems to be hemorrhaging facilities. As if they're a target of some malicious group. Like those animal extremists we put away a couple of years back."

"I'm not so sure. Think about it. Dubious experimentation with animal testing in Southampton. A suspicious death at Southampton *and* at Seahouses. A serious pollution case at Seahouses. An illegal gold mine in Wales *and* a suspicious drowning. And now this, blatant abuse of human rights and testing on illegal immigrants! Don't you see? Ananke doesn't look like a victim, rather more like a deserving target of retribution."

"Oh, I can see that, sir. But the means of that retribution, they don't appear legal."

"You're right." Pointer glanced out the hotel window. "Thank God, the sun's set. Let's have a meal and plan what we do next."

"Plan, sir? We haven't got..."

"All of a sudden, I've got a strong interest in the head of Ananke, Loup Dante. I'd like to know a lot more about him."

"What about Barnes and Gledhill?"

"Oh, we'll keep the alerts out to catch them if they trip up somewhere." He glanced at her. "Are the credit card companies are playing ball now?" She nodded. "Good. You're right. Their activities are still criminal. But I have a sneaking suspicion that the bigger fish is Dante, not Barnes or Gledhill."

"Sneaking suspicion, sir?"

He cocked an eyebrow. "Isn't that how they taught you policing?"

She smiled. "No, sir, they left that bit out. But since working with you, I've learned that a gut feeling is the best method in certain situations."

France

From this vantage point in the street, Brigitte Fornier had a clear view of the entrance to the graveyard. She pushed stray white-blonde hair from her forehead. It was a picturesque spot, a Provencal *village perche* overlooking the Riviera. But even beautiful scenery loses its thrall after a while.

Now, thoroughly bored, she got up from the wooden bench and paced the rough-hewn paving stones, her Nike trainers not making a sound.

She took out her cellphone from the pocket of her white tracksuit jacket and punched in her employer's number. "This is the third day, sir, and she hasn't turned up."

"I'm paying you by the day," Loup Dante said. "Paying you well, I might add."

"Are you sure she will come here?"

"As sure as I can be, yes. Keep vigilant."

"And the arrangement is the same as before?"

"Yes, Madam Fornier. Don't molest her. Simply follow her to wherever she stays overnight. Then, contact me and I will dispatch a team who will...deal with her."

"I could 'deal with her' for an increased fee. I've done wet-work before."

Dante sighed heavily. "I don't want her dead... Just follow her. Understood?"

"Yes, sir." The line went dead.

She shrugged. "You're the boss."

Chapter 18

Bear This Worthily

Cat's taxi stopped outside the fourteenth-century fortified gate of the village, the only access. On the journey here, she had reflected that her modeling career was over. The model called Cathy Gledhill must vanish without a trace. She was saddened because she enjoyed the work and loved most of the clothing and the people involved. Fine, sometimes the early mornings sucked, and a fair number of outfits were too outlandish to be worn anywhere other than a runway but it had been fun. So much fun.

Now, she traveled as Catalina Moreno while Rick was Ricardo, her husband.

When she told him of her intention of coming here, Rick pointed out that this village was close to Grasse, the perfume capital of Provence. He expressed a wish to visit with her. "Galimard and Fragonard have factories here," he argued.

"Sorry, *Ricardo*, but your interest in perfumes must lapse as has mine in modeling."

She thought that was the moment when it finally struck him that he was no longer able to resume his past life. He was willing to make this sacrifice for her. God, how she loved him for that—and so much else. When had it turned to love? Probably when she thought he was going to die in that mine. Her heart had pounded so much. She'd hidden her relief when they got out. Too bothered by that nasty piece of work, Jenkins, she supposed.

Rick smiled fleetingly. "A new beginning. Yes, few people are fortunate to get that, no?"

"The money Sol provided from those gold nuggets will help, I suspect?" she added.

"Yes. Happily, for obvious reasons, I kept a separate bank account from the one I used for my Ananke salary."

She had laughed. "And you call me paranoid!"

Now, as soon as she got out of the taxi cab, she realized her choice of shoes had been a mistake. The cobbles and stone paving were not ideal surfaces for her high heels even if they were strapped at her ankles. No help for it now, though.

She hefted the holdall over her shoulder and leaned in the front door to pay the driver. "*Merci.*"

As the cab performed a three-point turn and drove off, she made her way through the ancient archway and walked along the narrow streets, assaulted by heavily-scented flowers. She passed the shops and homes of many artisans, antique dealers, and a smattering of restaurants.

The heat of the day beat down on her head.

She was grateful that she had decided to wear a lightweight Madeleine tomato-colored jersey jumpsuit with a loose-fitting turndown collar, three-quarter sleeves, and wide legs.

The weight of the holdall began to tell by the time she sighted the church. She paused, pulled out the small plastic bottle of water, broke its cap, and gulped a good third of it.

As she approached, she noticed a blonde woman in a white tracksuit sitting at an ornate iron bench against a dry-stone building. She was in her twenties and seemed engrossed in her cellphone. Nobody else was in evidence; any tourists or villagers were too sensible and had elected to be indoors at this time of day.

Walking with care, Cat approached the entrance to the graveyard.

The cluster of gravestones was of assorted ages. Quite a few showed neglect while others seemed relatively fresh and tidy.

It took her about two minutes to get her bearings.

She stopped in front of the two marble headstones:

DEBORAH VIBRISSAE
(18 October 1958—4 June 1992)

DANIEL VIBRISSAE
(10 April 1952—11 September 2009)

To bear this worthily is good fortune. Marcus Aurelius.

Papa often read Aurelius' *Meditations*. The full quotation ran "So here is a rule to remember in future, when anything tempts you to feel bitter: not, 'This is a misfortune', but 'To bear this worthily is good fortune'." It was hard but she was thankful she had those years with her father. Many of the ancient Roman precepts fell in accord with her heartfelt beliefs but some did not. She could not settle for "Leave another's wrongdoing where it lies." No, never that.

This village was her father's birthplace. He told her that he and Maman visited during the summers. They found comfort here, among the tall golden houses that clung to the rocks and the labyrinth of tiny, vaulted passages and stairways that climbed up to the remains of the fortress. As her mother declined in health, when they visited, they simply settled on taking in the view and breathing in the heady scents of the colorful and exotic gardens.

Cat hadn't been surprised that they had both wanted to be buried here.

With a heavy heart, she lowered the holdall to the sward between the headstones and hunkered down to unzip it. She took out a small trowel and two little bunches of purple and white freesias complete with roots, her mother's favorites. She dug at the soil at the base of each headstone until she hit resistance at her father's.

When she had finished planting the flowers, she stood up and let the tears fall.

"Sorry it took so long," she whispered, "but I've finally begun to avenge you, Papa." She dearly yearned to quiz her mother about Loup Dante and the alleged affair. Her chest heaved. She sobbed and wiped her cheeks with a hand, noting that her fingers were smeared with earth.

She glanced over her shoulder.

As she had suspected, the woman in the tracksuit was watching her, now talking into her cellphone.

Cat patted the top of her father's tombstone and quickly lifted up the holdall. She made her way between the gravestones toward the rear of the churchyard.

As she reached the dry-stone wall that had clearly stood here for centuries, she peered back.

The woman on the phone stopped talking into it and gaped.

Cat removed the pack from the holdall and quickly strapped on the harness, over her shoulders, between her legs, and around her thighs. Her dress material was good quality and wouldn't spoil, she knew. She gingerly stepped up on the wall. Yes, the high heels were a mistake but she managed.

Spread out on her right was the sparkling sea and, beyond, distant isles. She turned and waved at the woman and then jumped out into space.

Brigitte Fornier swore and broke into an unsteady run, talking into the phone as she went. "She—she's just jumped—*jumped off the fucking wall!*"

"Wall?" Dante snapped. "What wall, woman?"

"The wall at the edge of the cliff!"

Brigitte arrived at the wall and stared.

Catherine Vibrissae, the woman she was supposed to follow, was in a free fall, her designer clothes flapping in the rush of air. It seemed as though she fell in slow motion. Then, abruptly, a parachute snaked out of the backpack she wore and it quickly billowed open, arresting her plummeting descent.

"She—she's got a parachute!"

Dante cursed.

After landing, with ease in a field by a road, Catherine Vibrissae smartly folded up the parachute.

A man pulled up his car, vaulted a fence, and helped her. Seconds later, they were in his car and motoring away.

Brigitte shuddered, contemplating the height of that fall. "I've lost her," she said.

"So I gather. Send me your invoice. Don't get in touch with me again."

"I..." She needn't bother; he'd closed the connection. Again, she swore. The crafty bitch, she thought, not without admiration. Vibrissae had known the graveside would be under surveillance, yet she came anyway. Why? What was so special?

She returned to the gravesite.

Beneath the freesias, the soil had been disturbed. Obviously. But it seemed as though more soil had been dug up than was necessary. The earth appeared a little sunken as if something had been dug up and then the soil replaced. But what?

She was reluctant to get her fingers dirty. What did it matter to her now? Dante had dismissed her and ended her contract. Sod him. But she wanted to satisfy her own curiosity.

Kneeling, her hands scrabbled away at the soil.

She stubbed her index finger and broke a nail but that didn't deter her.

Finally, she unearthed a small tin box, its hinges rusty.

She opened it.

Now, it was empty. But she was willing to bet something very valuable had been concealed inside. Why here, though? Didn't the wily woman trust safety deposit boxes?

"SAFETY DEPOSIT BOX KEYS?" Rick queried while he stood leaning on the balcony overlooking Nice Harbor. "Why did you hide them at your father's grave?"

"I don't trust bankers," she said, leaning shoulder to shoulder. "Not since the crash."

He chuckled. "Like lawyers, my love, they're a necessary evil."

"I know that." She glanced away at the sweep of the colorful marina spread before them. "When my father died, I was quite paranoid. I was reluctant to trust anyone."

He rested his hand on hers. "That's understandable."

She cocked her head and studied him. "It is, now I know that Dante engineered Papa's death."

"Can you really be sure of that? I mean, how'd that weird professor get wind of it? It can't be something Dante bandied about, can it?"

"Oh, I believe her. It fits. If my father had signed that agreement for rescue funds, his firm would have been saved—or at least wouldn't have ended up in Dante's hands."

"Okay. So, tell me, what's in those safety deposit boxes?"

She smiled. "When the time comes, I'll let you know. One thing at a time, Rick."

"One thing?"

She straightened up and tugged at his hand. "Come

on, I think we have some unfinished business to attend to in our room."

"What would that be?"

"Consummate our marriage?"

"But we aren't married," he explained reasonably enough.

"According to the documentation our friend Leon supplied, we are."

"I don't want to take advantage of—"

She planted a kiss on his mouth which silenced him. "But I want you to," she purred.

Author's Note

This novel was written and previously published in 2014 and was set in that same year. The world has changed considerably in the interim. I had thought of updating the book since eight years have passed and it might no longer seem contemporary. But that kind of updating is seriously fraught. And how often should a book be updated? Every year? In truth, a book becomes a period piece virtually as soon as it's published. Time does not stand still.

In the 1960s, Leslie Charteris' *Saint* books featuring Simon Templar gained a new popular readership in no small measure due to the TV series featuring Roger Moore. Yet a good number of the books had been published in the 1930s. Fashions, particularly women's, are often passé by the end of a season, car models come and go, and so on. Charteris had contemplated updating his early books but when faced with the immensely complex task, decided against it and asked readers to accept what might appear as anachronisms.

Similarly, I feel this story stands as it is, without

updating. One example might serve: since the events depicted here, the public house called The Harbour Inn on King Street in Seahouses has been converted into a restaurant called The Curry House even though its exterior appearance is very much unchanged. Other differences will occur as time passes, I'm sure: new roads are constructed, airlines go broke, flight times alter, getting faster—or slower.

Interestingly, this timeline fits nicely into Leon Cazador's adventurous timeline.

A Look At Book Two:

Catacomb

A suspenseful thriller with fast-paced action and intriguing characters…

A catacomb is a subterranean cemetery. A place where ancient corpses are found—or new ones are dumped…

After their recent success in Barcelona, both Catherine Vibrissae and Rick Barnes are continuing their crusade against Loup Dante and his global company, Ananke, by penetrating the lair of Petra Grimalkin in Nice. But death stalks the pair—as do the dogs of law from the British National Crime Agency—and when Cat and Rick's trail of vengeance leads them to the corrupt organization's health food processing plant in Northwest Africa, Cat comes face to face with an enemy from her past.

From the exotic streets of Tangier to the inhospitable High Atlas Mountains, danger lurks and deadly ambushes await…

Book two in the Cat's Crusade series, Catacomb follows a strong female character who is no stranger to deadly situations.

AVAILABLE APRIL 2023

About the Author

Nik Morton has sold over 100 short stories, edited periodicals and contributed to magazine articles, chaired writers' circles, run writing workshops, and judged competitions. He has edited many books and was sub-editor of the monthly magazine *Portsmouth Post* (2003-2007) and Editor in Chief of a U.S. Publisher (2011-2013). He has had 32 books published —including 3 books in the psychic spy *Tana Standish* series and 8 westerns—and co-written 4 books in the *Floreskand* fantasy series. His *Write a Western in 30 Days – with plenty of bullet points!* is a best-seller. With his wife Jennifer, Nik lived in Spain for several years (2003-2019). They have since returned to England, residing in Northumberland—near their daughter Hannah, son-in-law Harry and grandchildren Darius and Suri.